Even Annie's plans for a blue moon ritual had been shot down. That was something she'd been looking forward to. She'd been sure that Cooper and Kate would want to do it, too. But they didn't. They had more important things to do—things that didn't include her.

So do it yourself, she told herself. *Why do you need them?*

"Because we're a team," she said, as if she were really arguing with herself. "We're supposed to do things together. That's the whole point."

But Kate and Cooper didn't seem too worried about doing things together. They were making all kinds of plans that didn't include her. Plans with their boyfriends. Maybe it was time she started doing the same thing. *But I can't do that,* she thought. Then she paused. *Or could I?*

Follow the Circle:

Book 1: So Mote It Be
Book 2: Merry Meet
Book 3: Second Sight
Book 4: What the Cards Said
Book 5: In the Dreaming
Book 6: Ring of Light

circle of three

BOOK 7

blue moon

isobel bird

AVON BOOKS

An Imprint of HarperCollinsPublishers

Library of Congress Catalog Card Number: 00-109987

ISBN 0-06-447297-3

First Avon edition, 2001

❖

Visit us on the World Wide Web!
www.harperteen.com

CHAPTER 1

"With this offering of extra crispy I officially call this Friday night meeting of the Beecher Falls witch babies to order," Annie said as she set the bucket of fried chicken on the floor where her friends were sitting. "And for our vegetarian member we have a lovely carton of hot and spicy tofu," she added as she handed Cooper the bag she had just retrieved from the Dragon Dragon delivery guy.

Kate and Annie reached into the bucket of chicken and pulled out a leg and a breast, respectively, while Cooper rummaged in the bag.

"I don't know how you two can eat that stuff," Cooper commented as she opened the chopsticks that came with her order and dipped them into the carton of tofu. "It's death food."

"Yes," said Kate as she peeled a length of golden batter-covered skin from her chicken and popped it into her mouth. "But it's *really* good, and I'm sure the chickens will forgive us. After all, it is sort of their jobs, isn't it?"

Cooper opened her mouth to begin her usual diatribe against her perceived cruelties of the meat industry.

"I thought we agreed to not discuss our dietary philosophies on Friday nights," Annie said before Cooper could start, eyeing both Cooper and Kate sternly.

"I'm just saying," Cooper said innocently.

"Well, don't," Annie told her. "Just sit there and eat your bean curd."

Cooper gave her a mock wounded look and continued to eat. Annie wiped her mouth with her napkin and said, "Now that order has been restored, let's talk business. This is the first meeting we've had since class recessed. What is it we're supposed to do exactly?"

She tried to remember what Sophia had told them at their last class. Sophia and many of the other members of her coven and the Coven of the Green Wood were going to a Wiccan retreat for a couple of weeks, and several other people were going on vacation, so they had decided to cancel classes for two weeks. During that time the students had been instructed to continue their individual studies and, if possible, to meet with one another to discuss their progress.

"The big thing is our projects," Kate said, licking her fingers.

That was the other thing. Now that they were a third of the way through their year and a day of study, they were each supposed to come up with an artistic way to express what they had experienced and learned. They were going to use their first Tuesday night class back as a kind of talent show for everyone to present their projects to the rest of the class. Annie had been dreading it ever since Sophia had told them about it, and she had blocked it out of her mind.

"Right," she said unenthusiastically. "That, too."

"You don't sound real thrilled about the whole project thing," Cooper commented as she fished a chunk of tofu out of her carton.

"No," Annie said, trying to sound excited. "I'm looking forward to it. I just don't know what I'm going to do. What about you guys? What are you doing?"

Secretly, she was hoping that she would get some ideas for her own project by finding out what Kate and Cooper were going to do. The truth was that she really had no idea what she could do that might be interesting. She wasn't particularly artistic, and she was having trouble coming up with anything at all.

"You know we're not supposed to talk about it," Kate reminded her. "It's supposed to be a surprise."

"I know," Annie replied. "But you two have actual talent. I don't. I could use a little help here."

"You'll be fine. And you are talented. You're better at science and Tarot than either one of us," Cooper told her. "Don't worry about it."

"This isn't like science or Tarot," Annie responded. "I can't just do an experiment or look at some cards. I have to do something artsy, and I am *not* artsy. Kate sews. You play the guitar and write lyrics. What do I do? I *think*. That's not exactly going to hold an audience spellbound."

"You made that hedgehog head for the Midsummer ritual," Kate reminded her. Then she looked at Cooper. "Sorry for bringing it up," she said.

"It's okay," replied Cooper. "I've moved on." Cooper's experiences that Midsummer night in the woods had been very disturbing, and she had briefly left the study group because of what had happened. Only recently had she returned, and Kate and Annie were still a little hesitant to mention the events for fear of upsetting her again.

"One papier-mâché hedgehog head does not an artist make," Annie said. "But I have time. Let's talk about something else. How about progress reports?"

"What is this, parent-teacher conferences?" joked Cooper.

"Sophia told us to talk about how we're doing," Annie said. "So let's talk. We don't see a whole lot of each other these days. What have you guys been up to? Kate?"

Kate put down the bone from her chicken leg and sighed. "Let's see," she began. "Well, Aunt Netty went home this week from the hospital and she's doing better. Dr. Pedersen says her cancer has stopped spreading and now they can concentrate on getting rid of what's left."

"Have your parents mentioned anything about the ritual?" Cooper asked, referring to the healing circle the girls and their Wiccan friends had participated in a few weeks earlier in an attempt to help Kate's aunt in her battle against cancer.

"No," Kate answered. "They haven't said a word. It's like this big topic that we're all dancing around. I'm not bringing it up and they're not asking. As far as they know, it's just the two of you who are involved in all of this."

Cooper and Annie exchanged a glance. When the time had come to tell Kate's family about the proposed ritual, she'd told them that the coven members were friends of Annie's and Cooper's, and that she herself didn't really know them. It had been an innocent lie, and Cooper and Annie understood why she'd done it, but they both had a feeling that it was ultimately going to cause Kate more trouble than it had saved her.

"And what have you told them about Tyler?" Cooper asked, referring to Kate's Wiccan boyfriend.

"Nothing," said Kate. "They don't know he's a witch. To tell the truth, I'm sort of keeping him away from them. But he's been so busy working with Thatcher at his construction sites that it hasn't really been a problem. Plus, my mother is really busy with this big wedding she's catering, so there hasn't been a lot of time for question-and-answer sessions."

"So we've got Kate hiding her witchiness from her family and trying to keep her boyfriend under wraps," Annie said. "Cooper, how about you? Any subterfuge and deceitfulness in your life?"

"Hey!" Kate protested. "That's not fair."

Cooper held up her hand. "You had your turn," she said, grinning. "Now it's all about me."

Kate leaned against the bed and folded her arms across her chest, pretending to be put out while Cooper spoke.

"Well, you already know I sort of have a boyfriend now," Cooper said. "The band is kind of on hold for the summer, but I've kind of been thinking about doing some open-mike nights, performing my own stuff. There's a little one tomorrow night that I'm going to try out. But I'm not sure it's my thing."

"Why not?" asked Kate. "You'd be great at that."

"Yeah," said Annie. "You should go for it."

"I don't know," Cooper said, shaking her head. "We'll see."

"That leaves you, Annie," said Kate. "How have you been doing since Ben died?"

Annie instinctively looked to her dresser, where the picture of the elderly man she'd befriended at her volunteer job at a nearby nursing home had sat since Ben's unexpected death. "It's been sort of hard," she said. "I've been thinking a lot about death and all of that, and that's not all that much fun. I'm still going to the home every day, and I like that, but I feel like what could have been a great friendship was taken away from me before I could enjoy it."

She was quiet for a minute, and the other two waited for her to speak. Annie had experienced more than the usual share of death in her life, and talking about it was difficult for her. Since the deaths of her parents in a fire nine years before, she'd been reluctant to get too close to people. Apart from Cooper and Kate, Ben Rowe had been one of the only people she'd allowed herself to befriend since then, and his death had shaken her deeply, reminding her that people could be gone in an instant and that relationships could be wiped out before they'd even begun. She was still adjusting to the loss of Ben's friendship, and she wasn't sure she could explain to her friends how knowing him, even for just a few weeks, had been helping her get over losing her parents.

"It's just hard sometimes," she said. "But I'm okay."

She wanted to change the subject suddenly, to stop them from talking about Ben and death. Then she remembered something she wanted to tell her friends.

"Hey, what are we going to do for the blue moon?" she asked.

"The what moon?" Kate said, idly chewing on a chicken wing.

"The blue moon," replied Annie. "It's coming up on Sunday."

"What exactly is it?" Cooper asked her.

"Any time there are two full moons in one month the second one is called the blue moon," explained Annie. "It doesn't happen very often. You know, like 'once in a blue moon'?"

"Do we have to do something?" asked Kate.

"Well, I guess we don't *have* to," Annie answered. "But it's sort of a big deal. Blue moons are supposed to be good for doing special spells. I just thought maybe we could do a ritual or something."

"I don't know," Cooper said. "I think T.J. and I have plans for Sunday."

"And I've got to help my mother with this catering job," said Kate. "There's a ton of stuff to do. Besides, we did one full moon ritual already this month."

Annie sighed. "Okay," she said. "If you guys are busy we don't have to do anything."

"I'm sorry, Annie," Kate told her. "It's just that this catering job is really important."

"Who's it for anyway?" asked Cooper. "You're making it sound like it's royalty or something."

"Close," Kate said. "Lily Winter is marrying Jack Pershing."

"Lily Winter as in the daughter of Marshall Winter, director of the art museum?" said Annie, impressed.

"And Jack Pershing as in the son of Mayor Phyllis Pershing?" asked Cooper.

"That would be them," Kate confirmed. "Mayor

Pershing tasted my mom's cooking at a party she went to and then asked her if she'd cater the wedding. Mom is beside herself—the wedding is only two weeks away. They're holding it in the sculpture garden at the museum, and all these important people are going to be there. Mom has hired a bunch of extra people to help her out, but it's still driving her crazy."

"I've met the Pershings," said Cooper knowingly. "My father has done some work for the mayor. She's something else, all right."

"I'm going to be working a lot these next two weeks," lamented Kate. "So I'm not sure how much I'll even see you guys."

"And you're hanging out with T.J.," Annie said as she turned to Cooper.

"He's helping me work on some new material," Cooper told her. "He's really great for bouncing ideas off of."

"Okay, well, if nobody can do it I guess that's okay," said Annie. "There will be lots of other moons."

Kate and Cooper went back to talking about the Winter-Pershing wedding and about Cooper's first open-mike performance. Annie listened and tried to add encouraging comments, but inside she was thinking about other things. Mostly she was thinking about how much she'd been looking forward to doing a blue moon ritual. It had seemed like a great opportunity for her and her friends to work some magic by themselves, just the three of them. They hadn't done that in a long time, and now that Cooper was back it would have been a wonderful way to reaffirm their friendship and their magical commitments.

But now it looked like her friends had other things to do. Kate was busy with her mother, and Cooper was preoccupied with her upcoming performance. *And they both have boyfriends to think about*, Annie reminded herself. She didn't want that to bother her, but it did. Especially now that even Cooper had a boyfriend. Before it had always been Kate who talked about guys and dating, and Annie and Cooper had teased her about being boy crazy. They'd been sort of a team, the dateless ones picking on their more romance oriented friend. But now that Cooper was dating T.J., Annie was the odd one out. She'd never even been on a date.

And at this rate you never will, she thought miserably. She didn't even know where she would meet a boy. Kate had met Tyler at a ritual, but there were no other guys their age who came to those. And Cooper and T.J. had gotten together almost by accident. How was she ever supposed to get a guy? The only ones she met were the old men at Shady Hills.

"Maybe Tyler and I will come see you tomorrow night," Kate said to Cooper, interrupting Annie's moping. "It would be fun to hear you, and then we could all go out to eat afterward. It would almost be like a double date."

"That would be okay," replied Cooper. "What about you, Annie? Do you want to come?"

"I don't know," Annie said. "I don't have anyone to go with. A double date plus one extra isn't much fun for you guys."

"You have us," said Kate. "What else do you need? Come on. It will be a blast. We can heckle Cooper."

"Sure," Annie said after a moment. "I'll go."

Kate smiled and resumed her conversation with Cooper. *What else do I need?* Annie thought to herself, echoing Kate's words of a moment before. She wasn't sure, but she knew she needed something. Her friends were both happier than she'd ever seen them. But there was an empty space inside of her. Partly she knew that this was because of the death of Ben Rowe. But that was only part of it. His death had made her see that she'd been shutting herself off from even the possibility of getting close to someone. Not her friends, but someone who would be more than that. A boyfriend. She'd never even really let herself think about having one.

Not that you're pretty enough to get one, said that same nagging voice. She knew that wasn't true. Well, mostly it wasn't true. Sure, she wasn't a glamour queen or anything. But she was cute, and the one time she'd let Kate make her over she'd been really pleased with how she'd looked. She'd even noticed some of the guys looking at her in a different way. But no one had asked her out. No one had *ever* asked her out.

Maybe it's time to change that, she thought. But how? She couldn't just turn herself from a science brain into a hottie overnight. Still, perhaps it was time to try a little harder. After all, she was going to be sixteen in a little more than two months. It was about time she found out what all the fuss was about dating and, well, all the stuff that went along with it.

"Penny for your thoughts," said Kate, waving her hand in front of Annie's face and startling her back to attention.

"Oh, sorry," said Annie. "I spaced out for a minute. Um, I was just thinking about what to wear tomorrow night."

Cooper and Kate looked at her strangely. Then Cooper laughed. "It's just a coffeehouse," she said. "It's not the prom or anything. Wear whatever you want."

"Since when have you worried about what to wear?" Kate asked.

Annie felt herself reddening. She had said that about wondering what to wear simply because she couldn't think of anything else to say. "Don't worry about it," she said. "I was just thinking, that's all."

"Okay," Kate said. "Well, I should get going."

"But it's only eight o'clock!" said Annie. "Don't you want to watch a video or something?"

Kate shook her head. "I've got to be up early to help my mother," she said.

"I should go, too," Cooper told her, standing up. "I want to rewrite some stuff before tomorrow night."

They picked up the food containers and plates and took them down to the kitchen. Then Annie walked her friends to the door and said good night. Afterward she went back to her room and threw herself on the bed.

"Well, that was a lot of fun," she said aloud. "Eight o'clock on a Friday night and here I am by myself."

She was annoyed. She'd been hoping for a night of fun with her friends. A night like they usually had when they got together. But lately those nights had been few and far between. Kate and Cooper always seemed to have more important things to do. Even Annie's aunt and little sister had plans for the evening, going to a movie together so that Annie, Kate, and Cooper could have the house to themselves. But now there was no point to that. Annie was alone, and with nothing to do.

Even her plans for a blue moon ritual had been shot down. That was something she'd been looking forward to. She'd been sure that Cooper and Kate would want to do it, too. But they didn't. They had more important things to do—things that didn't include her.

So do it yourself, she told herself. *Why do you need them?*

"Because we're a team," she said, as if she were

really arguing with herself. "We're supposed to do things together. That's the whole point."

But Kate and Cooper didn't seem too worried about doing things together. They were making all kinds of plans that didn't include her. Plans with their boyfriends. Maybe it was time she started doing the same thing. *But I can't do that*, she thought. Then she paused. *Or could I?*

CHAPTER 2

Cooper sat beside T.J. at the little table, anxiously swirling the ice around in her half-empty glass of ginger ale. She was nervous, which surprised her. She was usually never edgy before a performance, or at least she never *had* been before. But now she was more than a little apprehensive about going onstage. Her heart was beating quickly, and she kept taking sips from the glass sitting in front of her.

"Relax," T.J. whispered in her ear as he slid his hand onto her knee and gave it a little squeeze. "You're going to be fine."

Cooper smiled nervously at him. *Easy for you to say*, she thought. *You're not the one about to make a fool of yourself.*

They were sitting in Cuppa Joe's, one of the coffee shops in the neighborhood around Jasper College. Normally it was filled with students who spread their books and papers all over the tables while they studied and wrote, or with people occupying the old sofas and armchairs that dotted the room. But tonight it had been transformed into a performance space. The tables and chairs had been arranged around a microphone at the back of the room, and a small spotlight made a bright circle behind the mike. The place was filled with people who had come to read their work and with people who had come to listen to them.

Cooper looked around at all the faces. It was an interesting mix of people, ranging from teenagers like herself to professors from the college, local artists of all kinds, and even a few business suit types who seemed wildly out of place in the casual crowd. Cooper recognized some of the people from past trips to the shop, but most of them she didn't. At least that made things easier. It was harder performing in front of people she knew. In fact, she was almost regretting having told her friends about the evening. But it was too late now. They were there, and she was about to go on.

She closed her eyes and went over the words to her piece in her head. It was short and she'd memorized it, of course, but she was suddenly afraid that she wouldn't remember the lines when the time came. It wasn't like lyrics, which at least had a melody behind them to give her memory a little kick when it needed one. This was a spoken word piece. She'd never performed anything like it before. She hadn't even *written* anything like it until pretty recently. This was all a little new to her, and while she was excited to be trying something different, she was nervous that it wouldn't come off the way she wanted it to.

She thought about her friends. Even though having them there was sort of stressful, she really was glad they'd come. Besides T.J., Kate and Tyler had come to support her. Annie was there, too, but she'd been very quiet all night. Probably she was still a little depressed about Ben Rowe's death, Cooper thought. At least she had come out with them. That was the important thing.

She opened her eyes and looked at the guy who was currently performing. He was apparently a favorite with the crowd, because they were laughing and applauding as he performed. *And I get to follow him*, thought Cooper, wishing she could go after someone the audience didn't like so much so that she would look great by default.

"When I see you with him," said the guy into the microphone, "my heart breaks open and my anger spills across the floor like those oranges that fell from the paper bag while we were running across the street in the rain after our first date."

He looked out at the audience as he finished, and Cooper was sure he was looking right at her as the crowd erupted in applause. Was he challenging her? *That's ridiculous*, she told herself. *He can't even see you in this crowd.* But still she felt as if he were daring her to be as good as he was.

The performer walked offstage and the host, a woman who doubled as a waitress, walked to the microphone.

"Thank you, Bob," she said as the applause

faded. "There's nothing like a bitter breakup to inspire you, is there, folks?"

People laughed. Cooper rubbed her hands against her thighs, knowing she was next. Suddenly she wished she'd never signed up for the performance. What had she been thinking? Well, it was too late now.

"And now let's hear it for a new face," the woman said. "She's pretty brave doing her first open-mike night in front of you animals, so give a hand for Cooper Rivers."

There was polite applause from the people around her as Cooper stood up. She walked through the tables and approached the mike, trying not to think too much about what she was going to say. She knew that if she did she would forget a lot of it. The best thing to do was to just launch into her performance.

"Why is it that little boys always chase little girls on the playground?" she began, looking out at the black shadows that were the faces of the people facing her. "Touching us and yelling 'cooties'!"

Now that she was talking, Cooper found that her mind had gone to that place it went to when she sang. She wasn't thinking about the words so much as she was feeling them. They came out of her mouth, a gift to the audience, and she let them speak for themselves. She felt herself becoming the person in her piece, the person whose words she was saying.

"If they're afraid that touching us will contaminate them, then why run by and pull our braids?" she continued. "Is it because they think they have to show us that they're stronger, faster, sharper? Or is it because they're afraid that if they don't touch us just a little that they won't be immune to what we carry? Like some kind of vaccination, maybe the teasing and the pinching are meant to keep them from becoming like us—weak, silly, slow."

She paused, letting the anticipation build as the audience waited for her to continue. The room was silent, and she knew they were listening, wanting to know what came next. That gave her a rush, and she launched into the final part of her piece with a lot of energy.

"But what they don't know is that we're not running as fast as we can," she said as if confiding a secret to her listeners. "We're *letting* them catch us. Because when they run off to wash their hands and boast to each other about how brave they are for touching us we stand and watch them go, laughing at their stupidity and knowing that for the rest of their lives they'll be trying to get more of what they've gotten on their hands. And we'll never give it to them."

She stopped, holding her breath. She could hear the gentle clicking of coffee cups and glasses. Then, like a wave crashing on the beach, those sounds disappeared in a flood of applause. She heard people

19

whistling, and she was pretty sure that her friends were calling out "Way to go, Cooper!" as she walked away from the microphone and found her way back to the table.

"Well," said the hostess as she stepped to the mike. "It looks like we have a new crowd favorite here tonight at the Cuppa. Let's have another round for Cooper Rivers. Way to go, girl."

There was more applause, and Cooper felt a warm glow fill her as she heard the sound. She'd felt it before, during shows with her band, but never for her alone. The people in the coffee shop had liked her words. They'd liked her performance. It made her feel alive, electric. The fear she'd felt was completely gone, replaced by pure joy.

"Cooper, that was just amazing," Tyler said when the applause settled down. "It makes me feel guilty for yanking all those braids when I was seven."

Cooper laughed. As the next performer walked to the stage, T.J. leaned over. "I told you that you'd be great," he said softly. "Good show."

She took his hand and squeezed it without saying a word. She was happy to have someone to share her excitement with. Then she looked over at Kate, who gave her a thumbs-up signal. Annie, though, seemed to be looking at the person who was about to go next. She didn't smile or give any sign that she'd enjoyed Cooper's piece. She just looked straight ahead, almost as if she were thinking about something totally different.

But Cooper didn't let Annie's reaction bother her. She knew she'd done well. The piece had come out pretty much the way she'd wanted it to. She would change a few things the next time she did it, but for a first time it was good, and she knew it.

There were three other performers. Cooper sat and listened to them closely, watching the way they moved and making mental notes about their styles. Some of the people were really good, while others needed some work. But each one of them had something to say, and that's what Cooper was really interested in. She loved hearing what people were thinking and feeling.

When it was all over and the hostess had wrapped the show up, Cooper turned to her friends.

"Anyone for food?" she asked. "I'm starving."

"Sure," Kate said, nodding. "Is that okay, Tyler?"

"Fine with me," her boyfriend answered.

"Annie?" asked Cooper.

"I don't know," Annie said. "I'm not all that hungry."

"Oh, come on," T.J. said. "If you don't come with us we'll be forced to talk about you."

"There's nothing to say," responded Annie sulkily.

"Then we'll make it up," Cooper told her, determined to not let anything ruin her good mood. She didn't know why Annie seemed so preoccupied, but she hoped she'd snap out of it soon.

Cooper stood up and the others followed.

Annie was the last to leave the table, and she hung back as they walked toward the coffee shop door. *But at least she's coming*, Cooper thought. She would ask her friend what was bothering her later. Normally, Annie would have been the first one to tell her what a great job she'd done, but she still hadn't said a word.

"Hey, I just want to say that your piece was really great," a woman said, stopping Cooper.

"Thanks," Cooper responded with surprise.

Someone else approached her—one of the guys who had performed. He reached out and took her hand. "Wonderful," he said dramatically. "Very inspired."

"Uh, thanks," Cooper said, pulling back her hand. "Yours was good, too."

"But nothing like yours," the man continued, clearly trying to make an impression.

"Ignore Trevor," said a voice beside Cooper. "He's a little wound up on caffeine."

Cooper looked over and saw that Bob was standing beside her. "He's right, though, you were really good."

"I think they liked your stuff better," Cooper replied.

Bob shook his head. "I'm not sure about that. But we'll see how it goes next time. See you later."

He walked off, and Cooper and her friends left the shop.

"Sounds to me like you're a hit," T.J. said as they

congregated on the sidewalk in front of the shop. "My girlfriend the performance artist. I don't know what I can possibly do to compete with your celebrity."

"Don't worry," said Cooper, playing along with him. "My publicist will find a minute or two every week to fit you into my schedule. And Kate, you can run my fan club. Tyler will be in charge of organizing the tours. Annie can be my personal assistant. See, it will all work out perfectly."

They walked down the street in the warm summer night, Cooper with T.J.'s arm around her shoulder and Kate holding hands with Tyler. Annie walked in between the two couples. Cooper was happy to be with her two best friends, and she was equally happy to have done a successful performance.

The group went into a restaurant at the end of the block. It was crowded with weekend business, but there was a booth in the back that they could all fit into. They squeezed in and waited for the waitress to bring them menus. When she did, Cooper was surprised to see that the person putting the menus on the table was Kate's old pal Jessica Talbot. Cooper looked at Kate to see what her reaction was, and wasn't at all shocked to see Kate looking uncomfortable.

"Hi, Jess," Kate said uneasily.

"Hey," Jessica replied in an equally strained voice.

Until she'd started hanging around with

Annie and Cooper, Kate had been best friends with Jessica, Tara Redding, and Sherrie Adams. Now she barely spoke to them, and Cooper knew that seeing her former best friend standing beside her waiting to take her order must be unsettling for Kate.

"How's everything?" Jessica asked. She very pointedly looked at Tyler.

"Great," Kate said, ignoring Jessica's stare. "How about with you?"

"About as good as it can be waitressing all summer," Jessica said.

"How's Tara?" Kate asked her. "I haven't seen her in a while either."

Jessica shrugged. "Okay, I guess," she said. "She hasn't been around much."

Big shock, Cooper thought. She knew that Tara wasn't around much because Sherrie had spread a horrible rumor about her right before the end of school. Partly it had happened because Sherrie wanted to get revenge for something Annie had done with Tara's help. None of them had seen Tara very much since. Cooper looked at Annie and saw that she was staring intently at her menu, obviously trying to ignore Jessica as much as possible.

"Tell her I said hi if you see her," said Kate.

"Sure," Jessica replied. "Now, what can I get you guys?"

They went around the table, giving their orders, and Jessica left. When she was gone Cooper sighed.

"And I thought we were going to have a Three Graces-free summer," she said. "Isn't Sherrie in France?"

"She's supposed to be," Kate said. "I don't know when she gets back."

"I wonder if she met the mysterious guy you told her she'd meet, Annie," said Cooper, referring to a Tarot card reading Annie had done for Sherrie at the school fair—the very Tarot card reading that had started all the trouble.

Annie shrugged. "I said she *might* meet someone," she said shortly.

"Well, I hope she did, and I hope he dumped her," Kate commented flatly.

"Wow, I'd hate to get on your bad side," remarked T.J. "Tyler, you and I had better watch out."

"You guys have nothing to worry about," Cooper said, patting T.J. on the knee. "As long as you give us everything we want."

Jessica returned a minute later with their drinks. As she was putting them on the table, her hand suddenly knocked against Annie's Coke and sent it spilling into her lap.

"Oh, I'm so sorry," Jessica said, grabbing a stack of napkins and blotting up the mess.

"It's okay," Annie said, dabbing at her sticky lap. "Really."

"I'll go get a rag," Jessica said, running off toward the kitchen.

"She did that on purpose," Annie said when Jessica was gone, picking at her wet clothes.

"I really don't think she did," Cooper said, handing Annie more napkins. "I think it was just an accident."

"Well, I don't," Annie told her curtly. "I think she did it to get even with me because she blames me for what Sherrie did to Tara."

"Jess isn't like that," Kate said. "Sherrie's the vindictive one."

"Well, it looks like hanging around with her has rubbed off on Jessica," said Annie angrily.

She stood up and brushed past Cooper and T.J.

"Where are you going?" Cooper asked her.

"Home," Annie said.

"What do you mean?" said Cooper, surprised at her friend's behavior. "It's just some soda. It will wash right off."

"That's okay," Annie told her. "I think I've had enough for one night. I'll see you guys later."

She turned and walked away. Cooper watched her leave the restaurant, then turned to the others. "Something's gotten into Miss Crandall this evening," she said. "She's been acting weird ever since we were at the coffee shop. It was like she didn't want to be there at all."

"Do you really think she's still upset about what happened with Sherrie and the Tarot cards?" Kate asked.

"I doubt it," replied Cooper. "I think it's something else."

"What's this about Tarot cards?" asked T.J.

Cooper sighed. *"That* is a long story," she said.

"We have time," T.J. responded. "Do you want to tell it?"

Cooper looked at Kate. She hadn't told T.J. very much about their involvement with Wicca. He knew all about her encounters with a ghost earlier in the year, and he knew that she attended the weekly study group with her friends. In fact, he had encouraged her to go back to the group after she'd left it. But they hadn't talked a lot about the subject in detail. This was the first time he'd ever really asked her a direct question about it. Was it time to tell him more? Although she'd told him more about herself than she'd ever told anyone besides her best friends, Cooper was still a little hesitant to tell him too much because once she started there was no going back.

Kate nodded at her, and Cooper knew she was telling her to go ahead. But should she? Did she really trust T.J. enough to let him know so much about what she did? She looked at his face. He was looking back at her with an open expression, waiting for her to say something.

She leaned back. "Well," she began. "It all started when we convinced Annie to tell fortunes."

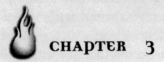

CHAPTER 3

"I've been thinking about the stuffed mushrooms," Mayor Pershing told Kate's mom at the pre–Winter-Pershing wedding meeting Kate was sitting in on. "Do you think we could have oysters instead? Diana and I discussed it, and we think they're so much more elegant."

"Certainly we could do that," answered Mrs. Morgan carefully. "But that will increase the overall cost dramatically."

"Oh, don't worry about that," the mayor said, brushing a piece of lint off the cuff of her navy blue blazer. "Just make sure they're fresh."

Mrs. Morgan wrote something in her notebook. "Okay," she said. "Oysters. Now, have you definitely settled on how many guests there will be?"

"We think it's two hundred and seventy-three," Diana Winter said primly, her clipped speech matching the crisp cream linen suit she was wearing.

"Two hundred and seventy-seven," her daughter, the bride, corrected her.

Lily was standing nearby on a short platform as a dressmaker measured her and made alterations to the beautiful wedding gown she was wearing. The seamstress was marking the hem while Mrs. Winter eyed her warily, her sharp features tense as the woman handled the ivory silk.

"Lily, I thought we agreed that the Simons and the Schusters would not be coming," said Mrs. Winter firmly, putting her well-manicured hands in her lap.

"No, Mother, *you* said they wouldn't be coming," Lily answered carefully as she played with the engagement ring on her finger. "I want them to attend. They're very good friends of mine."

"Two hundred and seventy-three," Mrs. Winter said again, turning and smiling at Kate's mother. There was a note of finality in her voice, and Kate knew that Lily had just lost the argument over the guests.

"That's forty more than I'd planned on," Mrs. Morgan said. "I'll have to order more chicken."

"Do whatever you have to," Mayor Pershing said, dabbing her mouth with a napkin. "This wedding has to be fabulous. *Everyone* will be there."

Everyone except Lily's friends, the Simons and the Schusters, Kate thought. She was sitting next to her mother on the couch in Mayor Pershing's impeccably decorated house. They'd been there almost two hours, going over and over the menu. Mrs. Winter and Mayor Pershing had changed their minds at least half a dozen times since hiring Mrs. Morgan to cater the affair, and Kate knew that they were driving her mother crazy. But this was a big deal—the largest event Mrs. Morgan had yet been asked to do—and Kate knew that it was important to her mother that her clients be happy.

"Oh, I almost forgot," Mrs. Winter said. "Dessert. The cake is going to be vanilla, so of course we want to have bowls of fresh strawberries and cream available. Will that be a problem?"

"But I ordered a chocolate cake," Lily said, sounding confused. "Chocolate is Jack's favorite!"

"Yes, dear, we know," the mayor said. "But your mother and I agree that vanilla is much more suited to an August wedding. Chocolate cake is for children, not for grown-ups, and it just doesn't fit with the rest of the food. I thought we'd told you."

Lily started to say something, but at a look from her mother she bit her lip and looked away.

"All right, then," said Mrs. Morgan, shutting her notebook. "I think that's everything. Now, just keep in mind that this is absolutely the last week that any changes can be made. So if anything else needs rearranging, call me by Thursday."

"I think this will be it," said Mrs. Winter. "Lily, do you have anything you want to add?"

Lily looked down shyly from her position on the platform. Kate had a feeling the young woman wasn't really enjoying making the plans for her wedding nearly as much as her mother and mother-in-law-to-be were. She'd spoken only a few times during the meeting, and then only to be quashed by her mother.

"It all sounds fine," she said softly, her hands running over the smooth folds of her dress.

"Good," said Mayor Pershing. "Then, if you'll excuse me, I have some work that needs to be done this afternoon. Diana, I'll see you tomorrow at lunch. Teresa, thank you so much for coming over today. It was lovely meeting your daughter."

"Thank you," Mrs. Morgan said. "It was a pleasure."

As her mother said her good-byes, Kate walked over to Lily. "Your dress is really beautiful," she said.

"Thanks," Lily said. "I wanted something more modern, but Mother had to have her way. I just keep reminding myself that it will all be over soon."

"Well, you look great," Kate said warmly.

She and her mother left the mayor's house and got into their car. As they drove home, Kate thought about Lily and the wedding.

"I can't believe that poor woman has to do everything her mother wants," she said. "It's *her* wedding."

Mrs. Morgan smiled. "Weddings are almost always more about the mothers than about the bride and groom," she said. "My wedding sure was."

"Really?" Kate said.

Her mother nodded. "Your grandmother wanted

everything to be just so. She planned everything, from the guest list to the color of the bridesmaids' dresses. And your Grandma Morgan, well, let's just say General Patton's troops probably had fewer instructions than your father and I got from her. By the time the day came we wanted to be on our honeymoon just to get away from them."

Kate laughed. "I can just see the two of them ordering you guys around," she said. "But you all look so happy in your wedding pictures."

"Don't be fooled," her mother replied. "We were just in shock."

"Why did you let them do it, then?" Kate asked.

Mrs. Morgan let out a long sigh. "Sometimes you do things to make your mother happy," she said. "I figured I would have the rest of my life with your father. It didn't hurt too much to give your grandmothers one day."

Kate thought about that. She knew a little bit how her mother must have felt. Although her mother very seldom insisted that Kate do something her way, Kate sometimes *didn't* do things she wanted to do simply because she knew her mother wouldn't approve. Like the whole Wicca thing. She was doing it, but she didn't bring it up because she knew her mother wouldn't like it. She'd even lied about the extent of her own involvement in Wicca when she'd suggested doing the healing ritual for Aunt Netty, her mother's sister. She didn't feel good about that, but she knew that telling her mother she was studying witchcraft wouldn't go over particularly well.

But would she stop going to the Tuesday night class if her mother told her to? She didn't know. She hoped she would never have to make that choice. In fact, one of the reasons she was helping her mother with catering the wedding was because she thought that if they spent more time together it might make her parents less suspicious when she hung out with Annie and Cooper. They'd made a couple of comments about how much time she spent with her friends, and she knew that it was because she'd told them that Cooper and Annie had gone to some rituals. But they hadn't asked her not to see them, and they hadn't asked any questions about what they did when they were together, and that was a good sign. Still, it couldn't hurt to rack up some brownie points by working with her mother. Besides, she enjoyed it. It was fun spending time with her mom and learning about the business.

"I haven't seen much of Annie and Cooper these past few weeks," her mother said suddenly, as if she knew what Kate was thinking about.

"They've been really busy," Kate told her. "Annie is working over at Shady Hills and Cooper is doing the tour guide thing at her house. Plus, she's got a new boyfriend, so she's been sort of scarce."

"What about Sherrie, Tara, and Jessica?" her mother asked. "Have you given up on them for good?"

The way her mother asked the question, Kate could tell that she was hoping Kate would say that she'd made up with her former best friends. Her mother had always liked Tara and Jessica, even if she did think Sherrie was kind of a snob. Kate knew that her mother had been concerned when Kate stopped hanging around with them and took up with Cooper and Annie. She'd never said anything outright about it, but Kate knew that she hoped someday the old group might get back together.

"I don't think we have a lot in common anymore," Kate told her.

"But you, Cooper, and Annie do?" asked Mrs. Morgan.

Kate nodded. "A lot more than the Graces and I ever did," she said, slipping and using the nickname she, Annie, and Cooper had given the trio of her former best friends.

"What did you call them?" asked her mom.

"It's just something we call them," Kate explained. "You know, the Greek goddesses of beauty and all that."

"I never understood what happened between you," her mother continued, ignoring the remark.

"It's a long story," said Kate. "Suffice it to say that Sherrie doesn't like it when she's not the boss."

"What about Jessica and Tara?" her mother pressed.

"Tara and I still sort of talk," Kate said carefully. "And I just saw Jess the other night when Tyler and

I went out. But I don't know. I think we've grown apart."

"Well, that's too bad," said her mother. "They're nice girls."

"So are Cooper and Annie," said Kate warily, not sure what her mother was getting at.

"Oh, I know," said Mrs. Morgan. "I'm not saying they're not."

"But you're saying *something*," Kate replied, testing the waters.

"I guess I just don't entirely understand what the three of you have in common," explained her mother. "They just seem a little . . . eccentric . . . compared to your old group of friends."

Kate knew full well that her mother was making a reference to the fact that she'd told her that Annie and Cooper were friendly with the people who'd done the ritual for her aunt. She knew that her parents still felt that what they'd done was weird, even if maybe it had helped her Aunt Netty feel better. And even if it *had* helped, they would never admit it. They would prefer to think that the medical treatments Netty was receiving were entirely responsible.

"They're a lot more normal than people think they are," Kate said, trying to not let the anger she was starting to feel inside creep into her voice.

"I know they were very kind about your aunt," her mother said. "And I really do appreciate that—"

"Yes," Kate said, interrupting her before she could start with the "but" Kate knew was coming.

"They were *very* helpful about that."

"I'm just saying that I'm surprised you're friends with girls like them," her mother said. "You've changed in the past few months."

"I like to think that I've matured," answered Kate, trying to sound like she was sort of kidding. But she wasn't. She really did think she'd grown up a lot since becoming friends with Cooper and Annie and beginning her study of the Craft.

"Yes, you have," her mother agreed. "But don't you ever miss hanging around with—"

She stopped as if she didn't know what to say next.

"With Scott?" Kate said, finishing the question for her. Her mother had never really asked about her breakup with her ex-boyfriend, and Kate had been expecting her to for some time.

"Not just Scott," said her mother. "Just your old group of friends. You used to go to so many parties."

"You mean I hung out with the popular kids," Kate replied.

"For lack of a better word, yes," admitted her mother.

"I didn't think you cared about stuff like that," Kate remarked.

"It's not that I think you need to be popular," answered her mother. "But you have to admit that Cooper and Annie are a little on the 'different' side."

"I admit that they aren't part of the Beecher Falls High School clique scene," Kate told her. "But that's one of the things I like about them. People who get their self-worth from being popular are the real losers."

Her mother smiled. "You *have* grown up," she said lightly. "I don't want you to think I don't like Annie and Cooper," she said. "I do. I just want you to be careful."

"Careful?" Kate repeated, feeling a tight, cold knot forming in her stomach.

"It's just that sometimes people who don't fit in sometimes have a hard time of it," her mother explained, speaking carefully.

"I see," said Kate. She knew that her mother wasn't really talking about her old friends. She was talking about Kate's getting involved in things she suspected Annie and Cooper of being involved in—things like Wicca. *It's too late for that*, she wanted to say. But instead she said, "You don't have to worry about me."

"Who's worried?" asked her mother innocently.

"So, how are you going to get all of this cooking done?" Kate asked, changing the subject.

"The museum has a kitchen," her mother said. "We can use that. And I'm hiring several cooks to help me out the day of the wedding. But there will be a ton of prep work over the next couple of weeks. That's where you come in."

"Just tell me what to do," Kate said cheerfully. "It's all fun."

Her mother snorted. "Let's see if you feel the same way after you've peeled six hundred carrots for the crudités," she said.

When they reached the house they walked in and found Kate's father in the kitchen. He was just putting the phone back on the hook.

"You just missed Netty," he told them.

"Should I call her back?" Mrs. Morgan asked.

Mr. Morgan shook his head. "She said she'd call you later tonight."

"Is everything all right?" asked Kate worriedly.

Her father nodded. "She's feeling great," he said. "The doctors are apparently amazed at how well she's responded to her treatment." He paused for a moment and then added, "She also was wondering if you could put her in touch with those people. You know, the ones who did the ceremony."

"The ritual?" Kate asked automatically. "Sure. I mean, I can ask Annie and Cooper. I'm sure they know how to reach them. But why does she want to do that?"

Her father sighed. "She seems to think that what they did had a big effect on her getting better," he said.

Kate nodded. She didn't want to say anything because clearly her father thought that Aunt Netty was crazy for wanting to talk to Sophia and the others. She was also worried because she wasn't sure how *she* felt about her aunt's talking to people from the group. She'd managed to keep her own involvement with them out of their conversations so far, but that would be hard if Aunt Netty started talking to Sophia more frequently.

She also noticed that her father was watching her as if there was something he wanted to ask her. She guessed that it was about the ritual, and she prayed he wouldn't ask her anything she couldn't answer honestly. Then she decided to distract him by asking a question of her own.

"So, who's watching the store this afternoon?" she asked. "You're not usually home on a weekend."

"Andreoli is holding down the fort," he answered.

"You left *Rick* in charge of the store?" Kate asked. "Isn't he the one who accidentally inflated the rubber raft and took out a whole display of fishing equipment?"

"I'm giving him a second chance," her father said. "There's some stuff I want to do around the house today. And by the way, right before Netty called your boyfriend called."

"Tyler?" Kate said. "Did he say what he wanted?"

"We didn't chat, Kate," her father answered. "Netty beeped in. He just asked you to call him." He looked at Kate's mother. "You know, maybe we should have Tyler's parents over for dinner one of these days. It would be nice to meet them."

Kate felt a shiver run down her spine. Inviting Tyler's parents over for dinner would *not* be a good idea at all. For one thing, they were divorced. For another, his mother was one of the leaders of the Coven of the Green Wood and his father was an ultraconservative who hated anything to do with Wicca. Having either one of them meet her parents would mean letting her secret out of the bag. There was no way she could let that happen.

"I'll mention it to him," she said as she left the room quickly, before anyone could start to make firm plans. "Maybe after all this wedding stuff is over," she added.

Great, she thought as she went to her room. *Now both of them are acting weird.* Her parents were definitely being more nosy than usual about her friends and her love life. Had they been talking about her? Did they have any idea what she was doing? She really hoped not. But just in case, maybe it was time to do a little damage control.

CHAPTER 4

Well, it's not blue, Annie thought as she looked out her window at the moon hanging full and round over the back garden. *But it is beautiful.*

She turned away and walked into the center of the room. She was mad. Even though Kate and Cooper had told her that they couldn't come over for a ritual, part of her had been hoping that they'd change their minds and call her that afternoon to say they were coming after all. She'd even waited for them, telling herself that they would manage to get there.

But they hadn't, and she was up in her room all alone, pacing and feeling sorry for herself. *No*, she thought. *I'm not feeling sorry for myself. I'm angry.* She was angry at her friends for bailing on her. She was angry because there were things in their lives that were apparently more important than getting together for a blue moon ritual.

True, blue moons weren't the most unusual things. It wasn't like they were missing one of the big sabbats or anything. Still, a blue moon didn't come around all that often, and it would have been nice to mark the occasion with a little ritual, especially considering that they hadn't done one together in quite a while. But no, Cooper was with T.J. and Kate was at home helping her mother. Only Annie was committed to making the time to do something.

The problem was that she didn't know what to do. A special moon called for a special ritual, and she wanted to do something that would make her feel better about being alone. She'd been thinking about it all afternoon and hadn't come up with anything. Now it was nine o'clock, the moon was waiting, and she still didn't have any ideas.

I suppose I could just cast a circle and meditate, she thought dully. But she could do that any time. This occasion called for something really interesting. Even if Kate and Cooper couldn't be there, she wanted to do a ritual she could remember, and maybe even tell them about to make them wish that they'd been there to experience it with her.

Only nothing was coming to her. She paced the floor for a while, walking in circles and thinking about what might be appropriate. They were between sabbats, so there was no particular theme to focus on. She didn't really feel like doing a spell. What else was there to do?

Frustrated, she went to her bookshelf and took out one of the books she'd been reading recently about different kinds of rituals and exercises people could do to strengthen their Wiccan practice. She flipped through the book, looking at pages at random and hoping something might catch her attention. But it all looked pretty boring at the moment.

Then, toward the back of the book, she saw an exercise called "Living with a Goddess." The title was intriguing, so she stopped and read some more.

One of the most useful and fascinating exercises anyone interested in learning more about the different goddesses (or gods) can do is to live with one for a while. No, you don't have to move to Mount Olympus or ascend to Valhalla. You can invite them to come to you. You do this by performing a ritual in which you ask your chosen deity to "stay" with you for a period of time—a week, a month, one cycle of the moon, etc. During this time you ask the goddess (or god) you've invited for a visit to lend her (or his) particular gifts to you.

For example, say you're feeling like your life is stuck in a rut and you want some help shaking things up a bit. You might consider calling on the Yoruban goddess Oya, who has been known to clean out more than one house by turning it upside down and forcing the inhabitants to spring into action. Ask Oya to come to your house and work her magic, lending you her powers of change and sweeping your life clean with her broom. Do a ritual in which you invoke her and ask her to give you some of her strength and determination. But be careful—make sure you *really* want her help or she might sweep you out along with the dust!

This ritual can be done whenever you need a little help from a particular deity, or simply when you want to learn more about a particular one in more detail. Many people say that by inviting different "houseguests" to share their homes and lives for a time they learn a lot about the various goddesses and gods and what gifts they have to offer. Just be sure that when it's time for the visit to end you send her (or him) away with your thanks.

Annie read a little more of the exercise. Although she'd been at rituals where different deities were invoked, she'd never thought about doing anything quite this elaborate before. It appealed to her. It would be interesting to learn more about one particular goddess or god, and it was something she could do on her own, without Kate and Cooper.

But which deity did she want to try out? There were a lot of them that interested her. The Russian witch figure Baba Yaga had always intrigued her, as had the Irish goddess Brigid, who was said to inspire artists of all kinds. Then there was Astarte, Rhiannon, and Ixchel. She'd read about all of them and had wondered how she could find out more about the goddesses behind the interesting names.

None of them seemed right, though. She wanted to choose a goddess who meant something to her, who had gifts that Annie wished she herself had. Who would that be? She thought for a few minutes, running through a list of names in her head. And then one leapt out at her. Freya. *Yes*, she thought happily. *That's it.*

Freya, the Norse goddess of love, had intrigued Annie ever since she was a little girl and someone had given her a picture book about the Norse gods and goddesses. Freya was beautiful, but she was also sad because her husband had disappeared. She often went looking for him in her chariot, drawn by cats, or by flying around in a suit made of feathers. When she wasn't doing that she held huge parties in her home, which was always filled with laughter and joy.

Annie had been intrigued by Freya's story. Now she seemed like a perfect candidate for Annie's first attempt at invoking a deity. She wasn't one of the more challenging goddesses, and Annie thought it would be fun to see what happened when she called on Freya.

Besides, she thought, *maybe she'll give me some of that famous beauty of hers.*

Now that she'd decided on a goddess to invite to spend time with her, she had to figure out how to do it. Turning back to the book, she read the instructions.

They directed her to decorate the ritual area in a way that the deity being called on would like.

What would Freya like? she wondered. She tried to remember details about the goddess. She couldn't remember a lot, but she recalled that Freya liked roses—pink and white roses. There had been something in the storybook about her having a garden of roses that she walked in.

I certainly have those, Annie thought as she smelled the sweet scent of roses drifting through her open window from the garden. There were a lot of roses in the garden. It would be easy to cut some of them and bring them inside. And she knew that somewhere she had some pink and white candles. All she had to do was get organized.

She jumped up, slipped on her shoes, and went downstairs. Her aunt was in the kitchen making herself some tea when Annie came in.

"Do you mind if I cut some roses from the garden?" Annie asked her.

"Not at all," Aunt Sarah replied. "Mind if I ask what for?"

"They're for a friend," Annie answered, grinning. She knew her aunt wouldn't ask any further questions, and she liked leaving her wondering who the friend might be. Suddenly she was feeling slightly mischievous, and she was looking forward to her ritual.

She took the clippers from their place inside a terra-cotta pot by the back porch and went into the garden. The night was warm and bright, and she had no trouble seeing as she went from bush to bush, cutting a few roses from each and placing them into the little basket she'd brought with her from the house. Soon the basket was filled with the beautiful flowers, and Annie went back inside.

"That's quite a haul," her aunt remarked as Annie walked through the kitchen with the flowers.

"It's a special occasion," said Annie teasingly as she went upstairs to her room.

She decided that the best thing to do was to just strew the floor with the flowers where she was going to do her ritual. She scattered them over the boards in a roughly circular shape. Their scent filled the room, perfuming the air, and delighting Annie's nose with the delicious smell.

Next she got the candles and placed them all around the room. She had almost twenty of them, and they covered all of the bare places. Annie lit them and watched as her bedroom glowed with their honey-colored light. The candles made everything feel very dreamlike, especially when the flames flickered in the gentle breeze and caused shadows to dance crazily across the walls and floor. Standing in the middle of the room, Annie felt as if she were in a magic forest. It was the perfect setting for what she was about to do.

She stood in the center of the ring of roses. Closing her eyes, she imagined herself surrounded by a circle of white light. In her mind she created a safe space where nothing bad could reach her and where she was surrounded by warmth and power. She pictured it filling her body until she was glowing with light. Then she held up her hands to the sky and said, "By East and West, by North and South, I cast this circle three times round. By Air and Water, Earth and Fire, I consecrate this sacred ground."

As she said the words she turned to each of the directions. She imagined the light in her flowing out through her hands, strengthening the circle as she spun slowly three times, each time seeing the circle in her mind grow brighter and brighter with the power of her energy and her words. After the third time she stopped and drew in a deep breath. She really did feel as if she were between the worlds, in a place where magic could flower and she could speak with whichever deity she called upon. It was a wonderful feeling, and she smiled to herself as she sat cross-legged on the floor in her sacred circle.

Okay, she thought, *now what do I do?* She hadn't thought much beyond casting the circle. Now she'd set the stage for her ritual and she had to come up with something for the main event. How exactly did you invoke a goddess? The book had said to call on her. Maybe it was that simple. She'd heard Sophia, Rowan, and other members of the covens she worked with do it before. What had they said? Suddenly it seemed harder than it had when someone else had been doing it.

She decided that the easiest thing to do would be to talk to Freya as if they were friends. After all, isn't that what she wanted to happen? She wanted Freya to come stay with her for a while and be her friend, so she might as well just invite her. She knew that while a lot of witches used elaborate invocations and flowery language, you didn't have to do any of that. Sophia had told them repeatedly that the gods and goddesses weren't some far-off entities hiding in remote placs. They were all around, waiting for people to speak to them. Annie had always liked that idea, and she herself had had several run-ins with Hecate, the Greek goddess of death and magic, when she was learning how to use the Tarot cards properly.

But that had been different. Hecate had appeared to her unbidden. Annie hadn't really called on her. This time she was actually asking a goddess to show up. Would she come? Or was Annie about to make a fool of herself? There was only one way to find out.

Here goes nothing, she thought. She had placed a single unlit pink candle in the ring with her. Now she lit a match and held it to the candle's wick, watching as it burst into flame. Gently blowing out the match, she laid it aside and gazed into the candle's center. She cleared her mind and thought about what she wanted to say. Then she began to speak.

"Freya," she said aloud, her voice almost a whisper. "Goddess of love, I ask that you come to my circle on this special night. Join me as I sit beneath the light of the blue moon. Talk to me. Answer my questions."

She paused, looking into the flames. She closed her eyes and tried to imagine what Freya would look like. There had been several pictures of her in the book Annie had read, and those came to mind. She saw Freya standing in a garden of roses. Her long golden hair fell around her shoulders and streamed down her back. Her skin was pink, with rosy spots on her cheeks. Around her neck was her famous necklace, forged from the brightest gold and sparkling with emeralds, diamonds, and rubies. She was beautiful.

"Freya," Annie called again. "Come to me. Be with me now."

She felt herself slipping into the semitrance state that often accompanied meditations. The room was warm, and she felt secure and happy. It was easy for her to let go. Then, suddenly, in her mind Annie thought she heard a voice speaking. It was gentle yet firm.

"I am here," the voice said. "What would you ask of me?"

Was it Freya speaking to her? Annie figured it was just her imagination. But it didn't matter. She knew that the most powerful part of any ritual or meditation wasn't what was real or not real but what the person doing the ritual wanted to achieve and what he or she got out of it.

"Welcome," Annie said to Freya.

"What do you need of me?" asked the goddess.

"I would like you to stay with me," said Annie, still talking out loud even though she knew the meditation was all in her mind. Somehow really speaking the words made it all seem more real to her. "I would like to learn more about you, and I would like to experience your gifts."

"What gifts might these be?" Freya asked her.

Annie had to think for a moment. She really hadn't had anything specific in mind. But now that the goddess had asked her, she found that there was something she wanted.

"I would like to have your gift of beauty," she said, surprising herself. But the more she thought about it the more she realized that she was speaking the truth. She was tired of being the one people looked right through. She wanted them to notice her for a change. Kate and Cooper got noticed, so why shouldn't she?

"Yes," she said again. "I would like to have some of your beauty and grace."

In her mind she heard the goddess laugh. It was a beautiful laugh, filled with light and love. It was exactly what she wished her own laugh sounded like, instead of the raucous giggles that usually tumbled out of her mouth when she thought something was funny.

"Very well," Freya said. "I will come to you for a time."

Annie smiled. She really felt like she was talking to the goddess. She could still see her in her mind, and her voice seemed clear, as if they were standing next to each other. She wanted to hold out her arms and embrace Freya like a friend.

And that's exactly what happened. She saw the goddess spread her arms and step forward, and the next thing she knew she was surrounded by the scent of flowers, vanilla, and cinnamon. She felt Freya's arms encircle her, pulling her close. Then it was almost as if the goddess passed into her. Annie was filled with a warmth, a contentment like she'd never experienced. Her whole body seemed to overflow with joy and happiness.

She opened her eyes and blinked a few times, just to prove to herself that she was awake and not dreaming. The entire meditation had seemed so alive that she was almost surprised to find herself still seated in the circle of roses and bathed in candlelight.

Had she done the ritual correctly? She couldn't really tell. While everything had seemed very real, she knew she hadn't really stood in a garden talking to Freya. Yet she *did* feel different. It was like something inside of her had changed in a subtle but important way. Some of the loneliness and anger she'd been feeling was gone, replaced by a sense of purpose. She suddenly felt as if she could do anything. It didn't matter that Kate and Cooper weren't with her. She had done the ritual all on her own, and it had gone well. She was proud of herself. And if Freya was around somewhere, all the better. Annie was looking forward to seeing what the goddess had in store for her—if, in fact, she had come at all.

She stood up and stretched, working the stiffness from her arms and legs. She had been sitting longer than she'd thought. Then she spun around, enjoying the feeling of being inside the sacred circle in her own room, with the full moon outside and the smell of roses all around. As she spun she reached up and undid the rubber band holding her long braid together. She used her fingers to comb out her hair, and soon it hung around her shoulders.

Stretching her hands out, she spun faster, her feet turning and her body swaying as she moved. It was making her a little dizzy, but she enjoyed the feeling. She was suddenly so happy that she laughed, and the sound was rich and pure, like water rolling over smooth stones.

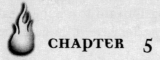

CHAPTER 5

"Is this Cooper Rivers?" the voice on the phone asked.

"Who's calling?" Cooper responded. She'd been wary of phone calls from people whose voices she didn't recognize ever since she'd received dozens of calls after the story about her being contacted by the ghost of Elizabeth Sanger had appeared in the paper. The woman talking sounded normal, but Cooper knew all too well that those people were usually the first to cause trouble.

"This is Sam Rogers," the woman told her. "I saw you perform over at Cuppa Joe's on Saturday night. You were really good."

"Thanks," replied Cooper, not sure what the woman wanted. Was she calling just because she'd liked the piece? That was nice, but kind of weird.

"I run the spoken word nights over at Big Mouth," Sam continued. "I was wondering if you'd like to perform at our New Words night on the ninth. It's a Tuesday."

Cooper didn't know what to say. Big Mouth was *the* place for performance art in the city. Everyone who was anyone in the poetry and performance art scene performed there. Now *she* was being asked to be part of one of their shows.

"Hello?" Sam said after Cooper failed to respond.

"I'm sorry," Cooper said finally. "Not to be rude or anything, but please tell me this isn't a joke."

Sam laughed. "No," she said. "It's not a joke. I thought what you said was really original, and your delivery was excellent. The New Words night is for emerging talent, and I particularly want to get more young people. So, how about it?"

"Count me in," Cooper said, trying to sound cool. She was about to burst with excitement, but she wanted Sam to think she was handling it like a mature artist.

"Great," Sam said. "Like I said, it's on the ninth. Be there around seven. We'll do all the advertising. All you have to do is show up. You'll have seven minutes, so you should be able to do at least three pieces. You have three, right?"

"Sure," Cooper said airily. *Not three that are ready*, she thought to herself. But Sam didn't need to know that. The performance wasn't until the ninth. That gave her eight days to whip her rough ideas into shape. That would be no problem.

"Okay then," Sam told her. "I'll see you on the night of the show. And once again, I really liked your stuff."

Cooper hung up. She stood in her room for a moment, staring at the wall and letting what had just happened sink in. Then she let out a whoop and started dancing around the room wildly, waving her arms around in a victory dance. She felt like an idiot, but she was so happy she didn't care. She had been asked to perform at Big Mouth. She still couldn't quite believe it was true.

What if it isn't true? she thought suddenly. *What if that was someone playing a joke on you?*

She stopped dancing. Was it possible that someone would do that? She didn't think so, but you could never be sure. *Artists are weird*, she reminded herself. Maybe someone from Cuppa Joe's was jealous of her, or just didn't like her, and had decided to show her up by pretending to be from Big Mouth.

Her elation faded as she looked at the phone, trying to decide if Sam Rogers was really who she said she was. Cooper didn't want to show up the night of the performance and find out she wasn't really on the bill.

Don't be ridiculous, she told herself. But the doubt was still there. Finally, after agonizing over it for a few minutes she went into the hallway and retrieved the phone book from the closet. Thumbing through it, she found the number for Big

Mouth and dialed it. She almost hung up, but before she could someone picked up.

"Is Sam Rogers there?" Cooper asked.

"Just a minute," the guy said, and Cooper could hear the phone being put down.

A few moments later Cooper heard someone say, "Hello?" It sounded like the woman's voice, but she was so nervous she couldn't be one hundred percent positive.

"Hi," said Cooper. "It's Cooper Rivers."

She paused a moment, waiting for Sam to say, "Who?"

But instead Sam said, "Hi. What's up?"

"Oh," said Cooper, realizing she hadn't made up any excuse for calling Sam back. "Um, I just wanted to double-check the time of the show. It's seven, right?"

"Right," Sam answered. "Just come on by and we'll set you up."

"Okay," said Cooper. "Thanks."

She hung up and once more began her celebratory dance, this time waving the phone book around while she did it. She was shimmying in front of the mirror when suddenly she looked up and saw T.J.'s face reflected in the shiny surface. She stopped dancing and whirled around.

"Hey," she said nonchalantly, as if she'd just been standing there checking her hair or something.

"Hey," he said. "Your mom let me in. Nice moves, by the way. You practicing for when you catch that big touchdown at the Super Bowl?"

Cooper knew she was blushing, but she tried to keep her cool. "No," she said. "Just having a little moment of artistic exuberance. I was celebrating my first major success as a spoken word performer."

"Two days after the fact?" T.J. said.

"Cuppa Joe's was just the warm-up," Cooper said. "I'm hitting the big time now."

T.J. raised an eyebrow. "Going on tour with Anastacia?" he asked.

"Better," said Cooper. She was dying to give him her news, but she wanted to hold out for as long as possible.

"Eminem?" T.J. tried again.

Cooper made a noise of disgust. "That malcontent?" she said. "Hardly. He should be half as talented as I am."

"I give up, then," T.J. said.

"You are looking at the star of the upcoming New Words night at none other than Big Mouth," Cooper said dramatically.

She was pleased to see that she had genuinely surprised T.J. He was looking at her with a mix of admiration and shock. "That is *so* cool!" he said.

"Isn't it?" Cooper responded. "I've got seven minutes. Now I just have to think of something to read."

"What do you have in mind?" asked her boyfriend. "You're not going to do the same piece again, are you?"

Cooper shook her head. "I want to do something different," she said. "I was hoping you'd help me pick some stuff."

"Sure," T.J. answered, sitting down on her bed.

Cooper went to her desk and pulled out a notebook. "I've been writing a lot of stuff lately," she told T.J. as she flipped the book open. "Lyrics, mostly, but I think some of it would work as spoken word stuff, too. There's a lot of great stuff in here about Wicca. I thought I might use some of that."

Since T.J. had asked about Annie and the Tarot cards on Saturday night, Cooper had told him a lot more about her interest in and involvement with witchcraft. After dinner with Kate and Tyler, he and she had taken a walk along the beach while she filled him in on what the Craft meant to her and what kinds of things she did. She'd told him everything about seeing Elizabeth Sanger's ghost and about the rituals she, Kate, and Annie had been to. She even told him all about the horrible events of Midsummer Eve.

T.J. had listened patiently, asking questions here and there when he didn't understand something. Afterward he'd given her a hug and a kiss and said, "I think it's cool you've found something like that to be into, but I like you because you're you."

Cooper had come home that night flying high. She'd never expected to find someone like T.J., someone who shared a lot of her interests and who let her be herself without feeling threatened or weirded out. She didn't expect him to become Wiccan or anything, but she was really happy that she could talk about it with him and not have to feel like he was judging her.

Now T.J. looked at the notebook in her hands and said, "You're thinking of talking about the witch stuff in your performances?"

"Yeah," Cooper said. "There's some great material here. I think it would be really powerful."

T.J. didn't respond right away. He had a look on his face that Cooper had never seen before, and she couldn't read it at all.

"Is something wrong?" she asked him.

"It's no big thing," replied T.J. "I was just thinking that maybe you could write about something else."

"Why?" asked Cooper. "It makes for good stuff. It's all about empowerment and embracing yourself. I think people would like it. Even if they don't, I like it."

"But your regular stuff is so great," T.J. said. "I think you'd do better if you just stuck with that."

"You haven't even heard my Wicca material," argued Cooper. "Shouldn't you at least hear some of it before you say that?" She couldn't understand why T.J. was being so resistant to the idea of her doing some pieces centered around the Craft.

T.J. sighed. "I just don't think you should hit people with that right at the beginning," he said.

Cooper put down the notebook. "Does it bother you that I'm into this?" she asked. "Because you said it didn't."

T.J. shook his head. "No, it doesn't bother me," he said. "I'm cool with it. But other people might not be. Look what happened when you talked about seeing that girl's ghost. You got harassed all over the place. I just don't want that to happen again."

"Thanks for your concern," Cooper said warily. "But why do I think it's more that you don't want people to think that your girlfriend might be a witch?"

T.J. groaned. "It's not that," he said. "It's hard to explain."

Cooper snorted. "Try me," she said.

T.J. patted the place next to him on the bed. "Sit down," he said. "I want to tell you something."

Suddenly, Cooper was afraid. What was T.J. going to say? Was he going to tell her that he didn't want to go out with her anymore? He'd seemed so cool on Saturday night. Had something changed since then? Had he been thinking it over and decided he couldn't deal with her involvement in Wicca?

Cooper sat down. "So talk," she said.

T.J. put his hands in his lap. "You know I have three brothers," he said.

Cooper nodded. T.J. had told her all about his family. His brother Mike, who was nineteen, was away at college. Seamus, who was twenty-one, lived in New York and worked as a bartender while he tried to break into acting. And Dylan, twenty-three, ran a construction company in Los Angeles. The McAllister boys, as they were known, were a tight-knit bunch even though they all lived in different parts of the country. T.J. was always talking about them, and although she had never met any of them, Cooper could tell that T.J. really loved them all.

"So you have three brothers," she said. "That's why you don't want me to do any witchy stuff at my performance? You're afraid your brothers might show up and hear it? *That* makes a lot of sense."

"No," said T.J. "Just listen for a minute. I haven't told you everything about my family. See, there's something about Dylan that you and I have never discussed. We don't even really talk about it at home much."

Cooper waited for T.J. to continue. She was still riled up over his suggestion that she censor her material, but he clearly was trying to share something with her.

"Dylan is gay," he said finally. Then he looked at her.

"So Dylan is gay," Cooper repeated, shrugging her shoulders. "What does that have to do with anything? Lots of people are gay."

"I know," T.J. said. "You're missing the point. *I* know it's okay for Dylan to be gay. *You* know it's okay for Dylan to be gay. But there are a lot of people out there who don't know that, or who don't think that. It took him a long time to tell any of us, and even then it took some people in my family a while to realize that it didn't matter. But there are still people he doesn't tell because it *would* matter to them. I mean, he's in construction. He can't tell every foreman and contractor and welder he works with that he's gay. They just wouldn't all understand."

Cooper took T.J.'s hand and held it. "I understand what you're saying," she told him. "And thanks for telling me about Dylan. But this isn't the same thing."

"I think it is," T.J. argued. "There are people who might not like Dylan if they knew he was gay, and there are people who might not like you if they know about the witch stuff."

"I don't *care* if people like me," Cooper said.

T.J. rolled his eyes. "As if I don't know that," he said. But then he turned serious. "It's not just about their not liking you," he said. "It can be worse. Dylan was attacked once by guys who found out he was gay and didn't like it. He was okay, but it really shook him up. It shook all of us up. You told me that you got a lot of nasty calls about the ghost thing. What if that happens again?"

"I got *calls*," said Cooper. "No one attacked me.

No one did anything more than call me a few names. They're not going to do anything worse this time."

"You don't know that," said T.J.

"Look," Cooper told her boyfriend. "I'm really sorry that something bad happened to Dylan. That shouldn't happen to anybody. But I'm not afraid of what people think."

"But what about what *I* think?" T.J. asked, looking into her eyes. "What if *I'm* worried about what will happen to you? Doesn't that matter?"

"Of course it matters!" said Cooper. "And I'm really happy that you care what might happen."

"Then don't do the witch stuff," T.J. said before Cooper could continue.

Cooper sighed. "T.J., no one is going to do anything," she repeated.

"I know you think you're this big tough girl," he replied. "But one of these days you're going to run into someone tougher than you are."

Cooper drew her hand back. "I don't need someone to protect me," she said, starting to get angry.

"Maybe you do," countered T.J. "Because if you keep talking about this stuff someone somewhere is going to hear it and start making trouble."

"And you're going to be the one to save me?" asked Cooper.

"You just really don't get it, do you?" he said, standing up.

"I understand that for some stupid reason you're

worried about people knowing what I do," she said. "Well, it's none of their business what I do. And if you really supported me you wouldn't care either."

"Maybe we shouldn't talk about this right now," T.J. said. "Maybe you should think about it for a while."

"I don't need to think about it," said Cooper. "I've already made up my mind. I'm doing the material I want to do."

T.J. looked at her for a moment, not saying anything. Then he shook his head. "I'm going to go," he said. "I'll talk to you later."

He walked out of her room, and she heard his feet on the stairs. Then the front door opened and closed. T.J. really had walked out on her.

Cooper wasn't entirely sure what had just happened. Everything had been going so well, and then T.J. had started to get unreasonable. Why couldn't he understand that she wasn't afraid of what people might think about her? She felt bad for Dylan and what had happened to him, and she understood that because of his experiences T.J. might be more wary than usual, but why couldn't he believe her when she said that she wasn't concerned?

This is why I never wanted a boyfriend, she thought to herself as she stared at the notebook sitting closed on her bed.

Well, it would be okay. She would give T.J. time to cool off and to see that she was right. Maybe she would call him later that night and try to talk to him again. But she still wished she had someone she could talk to about the whole thing.

Then she realized that she *did* have someone to talk to. She had Kate and Annie. She knew Annie was at work, but Kate was probably home. She picked up the phone and dialed her number, pleased that now that she had rejoined the group she could do such a thing.

Kate picked up on the second ring. Cooper immediately began relating her conversation with T.J. When she was done she finished up with, "Can you believe him?"

"Actually," said Kate, "I can."

"What do you mean?" Cooper asked.

"Maybe he's right," Kate said. "Maybe you would be asking for trouble. I'd really think about this before you do anything."

Cooper started to protest, but Kate said, "My mom needs me in the kitchen. I've got to go. But I'll see you Saturday at Annie's, right?"

"Sure," said Cooper.

"Call me if you want to talk," Kate said before hanging up.

Cooper put down the phone and stretched out on her bed, thinking. Was she crazy? Was she the only one who didn't see a problem with writing about Wicca in her performance pieces? Why was everyone so afraid of what other people might think? It annoyed her, especially coming from her boyfriend and one of her best friends.

Well, she couldn't let it get to her. She had work to do. Surely T.J. would come around, and so would Kate. They just had to get used to the idea. *It will be fine*, she told herself as she picked up her notebook, opened it, and started reading.

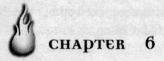

CHAPTER 6

Kate's mother put down the peach. "Order me two crates of those," she said to the man following along behind her. "Oh, and make sure there will be three crates of the strawberries. And *no* mushy ones. I'm going to hear it if they're not perfect."

"Will do, Mrs. Morgan," the man said as he made a note on the clipboard he was carrying. "I'll make sure everything is delivered by the afternoon of the eleventh."

"I can't believe those two are getting married on the thirteenth," Kate's mother said to her. "At least it's a Saturday and not a Friday. But still . . ."

"Look at you being all superstitious," Kate said, laughing.

"You can't be too careful," replied her mother, picking up a box of blueberries and eyeing them critically.

"Is there going to be anything else?" the man with them asked.

"I guess that's it for now," said Kate's mother. "Thanks, Paul."

The man nodded and left. Kate's mother turned to her. "That is, unless the mayor and the mother of the bride change their minds yet again."

Just then a muffled buzzing sound emanated from Mrs. Morgan's handbag. She reached in and pulled out a cell phone. Kate rolled her eyes as her mother answered it. She'd been teasing her mother endlessly since she'd come home with the phone, telling her that she was now just a Land Rover away from becoming one of those annoying yuppies they frequently made jokes about.

"Hello, Mayor Pershing," Mrs. Morgan said, and Kate suppressed a giggle. She wondered what the mayor wanted now. She called at least six times a day, and each call was about something more ridiculous than the last one.

"You've decided that you want the chicken in orange sauce instead of wine sauce," Kate's mother said. "Yes, I can do that. Uh-huh. No problem. Is there anything else? Okay then. Bye."

She clicked off the phone and gave Kate a menacing look. "They want orange sauce," she said. "Imagine that—another change."

"Just be glad they didn't ask to switch from chicken to veal," said Kate. "Mr. Reeves at the butcher's shop would be really irritated at having to send back a hundred and fifty chickens."

"Paul!" her mother called out, motioning for the

produce manager to come back. "Change that crate of mushrooms to two crates of oranges. Fresh ones!"

After the new order had been noted, Mrs. Morgan turned back to Kate. "I think we deserve a little treat after all of this," she said. "What do you say to lunch out? My treat."

"Are you sure we have time?" asked Kate seriously. "Mrs. Winter might call and ask you to change the wedding to a bar mitzvah."

"Come on," said her mother, laughing as they left the store. "I turned the phone off so they can't find me. I don't think even they can cause too much trouble in an hour."

They walked down the street to a little restaurant that had tables outside. From the table the waitress took them to, Kate could see everyone who walked by, which she liked. It was relaxing to sit in the sunshine and watch people as she studied the menu and decided what to have. She was trying to choose between the turkey club and the Caesar salad with shrimp when her mother tapped her on the arm.

"I *think* that's Annie coming this way," she said.

"You think it is?" Kate repeated as she turned to look. "How could you not know."

But when she saw who her mother was looking at she understood how she might have been confused. It was definitely Annie, but it was Annie as Kate had never seen her before. She stared as her friend walked toward them, unable to believe her eyes.

Annie had been transformed. Her hair had been freed from the braid she always wore it in, and it had been curled into long wavy tendrils that framed her face. And her face—Kate had never seen her looking so good. She'd once given Annie a makeover, but it had been nothing compared to this. Annie's lips were done in deep pink, and her brown eyes had been shadowed in tones of gold and smoke. Even her glasses were gone. Kate couldn't remember ever seeing Annie without them before. The change was, to say the least, astonishing.

Annie was even dressed differently. Her usual shapeless clothes had been replaced by a formfitting knit dress in a pretty pink color, and she was swinging a little pink purse by her side as if she'd carried one every day of her life, even though Kate had never seen her with anything other than her battered backpack. In her other hand were bags from several trendy stores Kate didn't think Annie even knew the names of, let alone shopped in.

"That *is* her, isn't it?" Mrs. Morgan asked.

"Um, yeah," said Kate. She waved at her friend. For a moment Annie looked at her blankly. Then she smiled and waved back. A moment later she was standing next to their table.

"Hi," Kate said. "What happened to you? You look great."

"I decided to give myself a little makeover,"

Annie said playfully. Even her way of speaking seemed different to Kate, less subdued and more outgoing.

"Would you like to join us for some lunch?" Mrs. Morgan asked. "We haven't ordered yet."

"I'd *love* to," Annie replied, pulling out a chair next to Kate and sitting down.

Kate couldn't stop stealing glances at her friend. The change that had come over Annie was remarkable, and Kate couldn't help wondering what had prompted it.

"Kate tells me you're working over at Shady Hills," Mrs. Morgan said as Annie looked at the menu.

"Yes," Annie said. "I thought it would be nice to volunteer there for the summer. I find the senior citizens very inspiring."

"Did you take today off?" Kate asked, noticing for the first time that Annie's nails had been done.

"Mmm hmmm," responded Annie. "I needed a little break. Besides, they had an opening at the hair salon so I took it. They're really hard to get."

"So I hear," said Kate, dumbfounded. Annie had never shown the slightest interest in hair or clothes or makeup. For a brief period after Kate's makeover she had maintained the look, but she had pretty quickly gone back to her usual mismatched style.

Annie put down the menu as the waitress arrived to take their orders. "I'll have the Waldorf salad," she said. "And a mineral water."

"I'd like a cheeseburger, medium well, with cheddar," Mrs. Morgan said. "And a side of fries, please."

"Ugh," Annie said, nudging Kate. "All of that fat. If I ate that it would go right to my butt."

She laughed. Kate didn't know what to do. Her mother was looking at Annie with a puzzled expression. Hoping to distract her, Kate ordered. "The turkey club," she said. "No mayo."

The waitress collected their menus and left. As soon as she was gone, Annie leaned over and said, "Kate, you should check out the sale at Banana Republic. They have the cutest blue dresses on sale there. I bet Tyler would love you in one of them."

Kate blushed. She saw her mother give Annie another look of surprise. Annie noticed it, too, and said, "Whoops. Sorry, Mrs. M. I didn't mean to say anything I shouldn't."

"It's okay," Mrs. Morgan said. "I'm sure you're right, and Tyler would be nuts not to notice Kate."

"Of course, he's not so bad himself," Annie said thoughtfully. "I mean, those *eyes*. Have you taken a good look at them? Wow."

Kate was really confused. What was Annie doing? She had never talked like this before, at least not to Kate, and certainly not in front of Kate's mother. If Kate didn't know better, she would have sworn she was talking to someone who just looked like Annie.

"It's too bad we don't have class tonight," Annie

said suddenly. "I'd love to see the reaction to my new look."

"Class?" Mrs. Morgan said, looking at Annie confusedly.

Annie nodded. "You know, our rit—"

She stopped as Kate kicked her under the table. What did Annie think she was doing? She knew Mrs. Morgan didn't know anything about the Tuesday night Wicca study group. Yet there she was, talking about it as if it were the most natural thing in the world.

"My chemistry class," Annie said as Kate breathed a sigh of relief. "I'm taking an advanced chem class this summer. But we're off tonight."

"I think if you showed up at a chemistry class looking like that people would be *very* surprised indeed," said Kate's mom.

"I bet you're right," Annie said. "Don't you think so, Kate?"

"I know you sure surprised *me*," Kate said, hoping Annie would get her meaning.

The waitress came back with their food, and soon they were all eating. As Annie nibbled on her salad she kept up a steady stream of conversation.

"So, what did you think of Cooper's perform- ance the other night?" she asked Kate.

"Performance?" Mrs. Morgan asked. "Did her band play somewhere?"

"Oh, no," Annie told her. "Cooper did a solo thing. She performed this really wicked spoken word piece. People loved it."

"She's doing another one next Tuesday," Kate commented, hoping she could steer Annie away from any potentially dangerous subjects.

"What kind of pieces does she do?" asked Kate's mother.

"It's hard to explain," said Annie. "You'd have to hear it. Then again, I'm not sure older people would really get it. It's kind of a younger generation thing."

"Really?" Mrs. Morgan said. "I'll be sure to wear my hearing aid."

"Oh, I didn't mean that you're old or anything," Annie replied. "I mean, you look great for someone your age."

"Thanks," said Kate's mom acidly. "So, you don't think one cheeseburger will put me over the edge, then?"

Annie shook her head. "No one expects women your age to have perfect figures," she said confidently.

Kate wanted to bury her head in her hands. Annie had met her mother several times before, and she'd always been her usual polite self. Now she was acting like an entirely different person. Kate knew her mother must be wondering what was wrong with Annie, too. Unfortunately, even Kate didn't know what was going on.

Annie took a few more bites of her salad and pushed the plate away. "No more for me," she said.

"Another bite and I won't be able to fit into this dress."

She looked at her watch and gasped. "I almost forgot," she said. "I have to go. I have an appointment at the tanning salon in fifteen minutes."

She gathered up her bags and her purse. "Thanks so much for lunch," she said to Mrs. Morgan. "It was great seeing you." Then she leaned over and gave Kate a little kiss on the cheek. "Bye, darling," she said. "I'll give you a call later."

She scurried away from the restaurant, waving good-bye again when she reached the corner. As soon as she was gone Kate's mother gave her daughter a look of utter shock.

"Was that the same girl I've met before?" she asked. "You don't by any chance have *two* friends named Annie and I'm just confusing them?"

"I'm wondering the same thing," Kate responded. "I've never seen her look like that or heard her talk like that. I don't know what's gotten into her."

"Well, *something* sure has," Mrs. Morgan said. "Maybe it's this chemistry class she's taking."

By the way her mother said the words "chemistry class," Kate knew that she hadn't bought Annie's story. Did she have any idea what Annie was really up to? Kate didn't think there was any way she could. But maybe she'd heard enough to make a pretty good guess.

"The last time I saw Annie was at the hospital when her friends did that ceremony for Netty,"

Kate's mother said as if she were thinking carefully. "She sure didn't look like that then."

Kate understood what her mother was implying—that somehow Annie's involvement with Sophia and the others was the cause of her transformation. Kate knew that wasn't true, but she couldn't say so without exposing the fact that she herself was also involved with them. She was backed into a corner, and she wasn't sure how to get out of it.

"I think she's reacting to the death of the man she met at Shady Hills," she said finally. "You know, she took that really hard. Maybe this is just her way of trying to snap out of it."

Mrs. Morgan raised one eyebrow. "So the next time I'm feeling down I should squeeze myself into a slinky little number?" she asked.

"It wasn't that bad," countered Kate. "I thought she looked nice."

"Don't you mean you think maybe Tyler would like you in it?" asked her mother.

Kate groaned. "She didn't mean anything by that," she said.

Mrs. Morgan smiled at her daughter. "Don't worry," she said. "I'm not going to give you the third degree or anything. But this hasn't exactly made me feel better about Cooper and Annie as your new friends."

Kate didn't respond. She had to admit that if she were in her mother's position she would probably think the same thing. Annie *had* been acting very strangely, and Kate had no explanation for why. And she couldn't go to her friend's defense because that would mean talking about issues she didn't want to talk about with her mother. So she sat there, picking at her turkey club and wishing they'd never seen Annie.

"Annie lives with her aunt, right?" Mrs. Morgan asked.

"Yes," Kate answered. "She and her sister have lived there since their parents died."

Her mother nodded knowingly. "She's probably just rebelling," she said.

Kate laughed. The idea of Annie rebelling against anything was almost comical. She was the most by-the-book person Kate knew. Cooper was the rebellious one. *Maybe that's the problem*, she thought suddenly. *Maybe Annie is trying to be more like Cooper.* She thought back to the night of the reading. Annie had seemed very distant, almost like a little kid who was trying to get attention by pretending to not care about what was going on. She'd seemed almost jealous of Cooper, and she'd run out of the restaurant quickly after Jessica had spilled the soda on her.

"You might be right," she told her mother. "Cooper was getting all the attention the other night. Maybe Annie is just trying to step into the spotlight for a change."

But even as she said it she wasn't sure that was

the whole story. It wasn't just Annie's looks that had changed. Her whole attitude was different. She was confident to the point of being rude, and she seemed to have an aura of glamour that Kate would never have thought her capable of. *She seemed almost sexy*, Kate thought. "Sexy" and "Annie" were two words that just did not go together. Whatever was going on with her, the explanation had to be more than just a makeover to boost her self-esteem.

As Kate was thinking everything over, the waitress arrived to clear their plates. "Can I interest you in any dessert this afternoon?" she asked. "We have a great strawberry tart."

"Don't even talk to me about strawberries," Mrs. Morgan joked. "I'm going to have about three thousand of them in my kitchen before too long."

"How about some sorbet?" suggested the waitress.

"Nothing for me," Kate's mother replied. "Apparently I'm teetering on the brink of obesity and have to watch my weight."

"Nothing for me either," Kate told the waitress, who put down the check and left with the dishes.

Mrs. Morgan fished in her purse for her wallet and left some money on the table. Then she switched on her cell phone. Immediately there was a beep indicating that she had a message waiting.

"I wonder who that could be?" she said sarcastically as she dialed.

Kate watched as her mother listened to her

messages. She herself was wondering what to do about Annie. Should she say anything to her about her behavior, or should she just let it go? Should she tell Cooper about it? *It's probably just temporary*, she told herself. *It's nothing to worry about.*

Her mother finished reviewing her messages and hung up. "There were four calls," she said. "Two from each of them. Apparently now we're having chilled shrimp instead of oysters, asparagus instead of green beans, red *and* white wine, and six more people for dinner."

"Is *that* all?" Kate said.

"Come on, Miss Smarty Pants," her mother said as she stood up. "We'd better get back to the fish market and tell Mr. Elliott to cancel the oysters and load up on shrimp. I hope he hasn't already put in a call for them, or we'll be stuck eating oyster stew for a month."

"Look on the bright side," Kate said as they left the restaurant. "You might get a nice pearl necklace out of it."

CHAPTER 7

Annie was feeling really good. *And you're looking good, too,* she told herself as she checked out her appearance in the mirror of the store's dressing room. The sweater she was trying on looked perfect with the skirt she'd just bought at the store next door, and she was pleased that she'd put together such a great outfit. She was even getting used to the contact lenses she'd been wearing. She'd had them for a while, ever since her aunt had suggested she try them, but poking them in her eye had always freaked her out and she'd stuck with her glasses. Now, though, she liked not having to push her glasses up her nose every five minutes.

I have to remember to call Kate back, she reminded herself as she fixed her hair. Her friend had called the night before, but Annie had been out. It had been fun seeing Kate and her mom at lunch. In fact, just about everything seemed like fun since she'd done her blue moon ritual. She didn't know why, exactly, but it had filled her with a new sense of just how great life could be. Asking Freya for some help had been a fab idea. Even her work at Shady Hills had become more interesting. Just that afternoon Mrs. Abercrombie had remarked about how good Annie looked and how happy she seemed, and many of the patients had made comments as well.

I am happy, Annie thought, taking off the sweater and skirt and putting her other clothes back on. Now that she thought about it, she realized that she'd almost totally shaken the funk she'd been in ever since Ben's death. She still missed him, but she realized now that she couldn't sit around waiting for life to get interesting. She had to *make* it interesting.

Cooper and Kate aren't the only ones who can be cool, she thought as she walked out of the dressing room to pay for the sweater. She'd enjoyed the look of surprise on Kate's face when she'd seen the new and improved Annie. She knew that no one ever expected her to do anything daring or different. She was always safe, predictable Annie. Well not anymore. Things were changing, and she was a new girl.

"That's a great sweater," the salesclerk said as she rang up Annie's purchase and put it into a bag.

"Yeah, if you like to wear *last* year's styles," said a voice behind Annie.

Annie turned around and saw Sherrie standing behind her with Jessica. Sherrie had a smirk on her face as she looked Annie up and down.

"Going for the Drew Barrymore look or something?" Sherrie asked, laughing derisively.

Annie ignored the comment. "Back from Paris already, Sherrie?" she asked calmly. "What happened, did you use up all the phrases you could remember from French class on the first day? Or did your parents just run out of money?"

Jessica smiled, and Annie felt a thrill of excitement run through her. She'd just gotten off a good one at Sherrie's expense. Sherrie knew it, too, and her face darkened.

"Don't think you can put on some new clothes and a little makeup and be a new person," she snapped. "Inside that tacky dress there's still a glasses-wearing little brainiac freak."

"Oh, Sherrie," Annie said in a sincere voice as she touched one hand lightly to her chest. "I'm so sorry. I didn't mean to upset you. I know how hard it must be for you to deal with the horror of bad hair." She looked meaningfully at Sherrie's head, which sported a new 'do.

"I'll have you know this was done in one of the best salons in Paris," Sherrie said, glaring at her.

"Really?" Annie replied. "Do they normally groom poodles?"

The girl behind the counter laughed out loud. Sherrie cut her eyes at her and the girl stopped. But the damage had been done, and Annie knew that Sherrie was on the verge of exploding.

"Just who do you think you are?" Sherrie said. "Some little nobody who nobody likes and nobody cares about. You wouldn't know the first thing about style."

Annie paused, pretending to consider what Sherrie had just said. Then she cleared her throat. "Tell me, Sherrie," she said. "Did you grow up wanting to be a total waste of space, or was it just something you fell into when you realized that the whole modeling thing probably wasn't going to work out?"

Sherrie was speechless for a moment. There was an awful silence as she stood there, shaking with rage. Behind her, Jessica couldn't hold back the smile that was trying to break out on her face, and the salesgirl had to pretend to be concentrating on folding shirts at a nearby table to keep from laughing out loud.

"You . . ." Sherrie said. "You . . . You little—"

"Witch?" Annie said, cocking her head. "Isn't that the word you're searching through your tiny little brain for, Sherrie?"

The other girl's face was bright red with anger. Annie knew she'd never been spoken to in such a way. She also knew that Sherrie really *had* wanted to call her a witch. Several times Sherrie had suggested that Annie, Kate, and Cooper might be hiding something, but she'd never come right out and said it. Annie knew that by saying it for her she'd robbed Sherrie of something she'd thought of as a weapon.

That made her elation all the more enjoyable. She stood her ground, watching Sherrie grow more and more upset.

"You wait until I get through with you," Sherrie said finally, her voice shaking.

"I think you've got something wrong," Annie replied. "You *are* through with me. There's nothing you can throw at me that I can't handle, Sherrie. And the harder you throw, the harder I'll throw right back."

Jessica was looking at Annie with an expression of shock and glee. Annie reveled in it, knowing that, like Tara, Jessica was probably sick of Sherrie's behavior, too. Maybe this would be the thing that finally got her to break away from Sherrie. Annie hoped so. She knew that would be one more thing that would drive Sherrie crazy.

"What are you going to do?" Sherrie spat at her. "Make me disappear? Maybe make me go away like your parents did?"

Annie felt her hand move before she knew she was doing it. Her palm connected with Sherrie's cheek, and the sound of the slap echoed through the store. Sherrie's head whipped to the side, and when Annie pulled her hand back she saw a bright red welt rising up on the other girl's skin. Her own palm stung, but it was a delicious kind of pain. She'd never felt anything like it. She'd never felt so full of pure, focused power.

Jessica's mouth had dropped open. Over at the

table, the salesgirl was standing, a half-folded shirt in her hands, as she kept her eyes on the scene being played out a few feet away. Nobody was moving. They'd all been frozen, transfixed by what had just occurred. Annie continued to stare at Sherrie, who was now pressing her hand to her cheek and looking as if she didn't know what had just happened.

"That's your first strike, Sherrie," Annie said calmly. "Two more and you're out. Got it?"

She turned, plucked her bag from the counter, and walked away. She knew that everyone was staring after her, and she was glad that they were. She wanted them to remember her, and she wanted them to remember what she'd done. She just wished *more* people who knew Sherrie had been there to witness her comeuppance. She wished Cooper and Kate could have seen it. But she could tell them about it later. For now she had the satisfaction of knowing that she'd bested Sherrie once and for all.

She strolled down the street, trying to decide what to do next. She could shop some more, but she had everything she needed. She could go home. It was nearing time for dinner, and she'd promised her aunt and Meg that she would make her famous burritos for them that night. But she didn't need to rush for that. She could take her time. She'd discovered a new joy in just walking down the street since she'd developed her new attitude about life. She liked looking at people, and she liked it when they looked at her.

As she passed a record store she peered in the window and remembered that she wanted to look for something. She pushed the door open and went inside. Then she headed for the jazz CDs. Recently her aunt had been playing some music that Annie had really liked. When she'd asked who it was, Aunt Sarah had told her that it was a singer named Sarah Vaughan. Annie had liked her voice. It was smoky and sweet at the same time. Plus the songs had been great, elegant and soulful, unlike the stuff she heard on the radio now. Most of all the music reminded her of her mother, who had often played jazz music while she worked. Annie wanted to get some CDs so she could play them in her room.

She went to the jazz section and began looking through the CDs. She didn't really know anything about jazz, so she wasn't sure what she was looking for. She tried to remember the names of the singers her mother had liked, but she couldn't come up with any. She did find the Sarah Vaughan CDs, though, and she looked through them trying to decide which one she should get.

"Do you need any help?" someone asked, making her look up.

A guy was standing beside her. He was smiling and looking at her appreciatively. Annie smiled back. He was cute, she thought—tall, with sandy brown hair and blue eyes.

"I'm not exactly sure what I want," she said.

"Do you like jazz?" he asked.

She nodded. "I just don't know a lot about it. Do you?"

"Well," he said. "Not as much as I know about blues, but enough to help you out. What are you looking for?"

"I was thinking about Sarah Vaughan," Annie said. She couldn't help noticing that the guy was looking as much at her as he was at the CDs.

"She's certainly one of the greats," he told her as he scanned the selection. "A lot of people prefer Ella Fitzgerald, but I happen to like Vaughan better. Have you tried this one?"

He held up a CD. Annie glanced at the cover. "I don't really know," she said. "I just heard someone playing her and I liked her."

"Well, this is a great one to start with," the guy said, handing it to her.

"Thanks," said Annie, pushing her hair behind her ear.

"No problem. And can I recommend something else?"

"Sure," Annie said. She was enjoying the attention the salesclerk was paying to her, and she was happy to follow him as he led her to the next row of CDs.

"This is one of my favorites," he said, handing her another disc. "It's a singer named Cassandra Wilson. She's more contemporary than Vaughan, but if you like that sound I think you'll like this one."

Annie looked at the CD, trying to decide if she wanted to buy it or not.

"If you don't like it you can bring it back," said the clerk. "What have you got to lose?"

"Nothing," Annie said lightly. "I'll take it."

She followed the guy to the counter. As he totaled up her CDs he looked at her and smiled again. "I'm Brian, by the way," he said.

"Annie," replied Annie.

"I must say, we don't get a lot of people your age coming in here and buying jazz," Brian commented.

"My age?" Annie said. "You don't look much older than I am."

"I'm seventeen," Brian told her.

"Only a year older than me," replied Annie. Actually, Brian was a year and a few months older, but he didn't need to know that. Fifteen sounded too young. Sixteen seemed more sophisticated.

"You don't go to Beecher Falls High, though," Annie said. "I'd remember seeing you if you did." She couldn't believe she was being so flirtatious. It wasn't like her at all. Normally she would freeze up if a guy talked to her.

"I will in the fall," Brian answered. "My folks just moved here at the end of the school year. I'll be a senior."

"That's rough, spending your senior year in a new school," said Annie.

"Tell me about it," Brian said, snorting. "I would

have done anything to stay in my old place. But what can you do?"

"Well, now you have at least one friend here. I'll be a junior at BFHS," Annie said warmly.

Brian grinned. "Thanks," he said. "I'm glad you stopped in."

"Me, too," Annie responded. "Thanks for the CD suggestion. I'll let you know what I think."

She turned and walked toward the door.

"Hey," Brian called after her.

Annie looked back. "Did I forget my receipt?" she asked.

"No," said Brian. "I just didn't want you to walk out before I could ask you if you wanted to go out sometime."

Annie paused. She didn't know what to say. Had Brian really just asked her out? She thought so, but she couldn't quite believe it. No one had ever asked her out before. Now that someone had, she wasn't sure how she was supposed to respond. But as she expected to fumble for the words to say, she found that they came easily to her. It was as if a hidden part of her opened up, a part that knew all about how to handle guys.

"So ask," she said.

Brian looked taken aback. Then he smiled. "Would you like to go out sometime?"

"I think I'd like that a lot," said Annie, surprised at how confident she sounded. "What did you have in mind?"

Brian shrugged. "I'm the new guy," he said. "I don't really know the city. To tell the truth, I hadn't thought that far ahead. I was just sort of working on the asking-you-out part."

Annie liked how nervous Brian sounded. Normally she was the one who was at a loss for what to say. But now this guy was asking her out and he sounded like *he* was the one who didn't know what to do. It was a refreshing feeling to be in control.

"Why don't we start with dinner?" she suggested. "Friday night?"

Brian nodded. "Okay," he said. Then he was quiet again, and Annie realized he was trying to think of a place to suggest for dinner.

"Grendel's is a nice place," she said, helping him out. "Casual, and they have great food."

"Grendel's it is," Brian said, sounding relieved. "Is seven okay?"

"Seven is perfect," replied Annie, writing her phone number down for him. "I'll meet you there. You *can* find it, right?"

"Sure," Brian said. "No problem."

She waved good-bye and left. As she walked out, she knew that Brian was still watching her, and she had to keep herself from doing a jump for joy. A guy had asked her out! And not just any guy—a *cute* guy. She hadn't wanted to seem too interested, but she'd had a hard time not staring back at Brian. His eyes were gorgeous, and the rest of him wasn't bad either.

Thanks, Freya, she said as she walked to the bus stop. *I don't know what you're doing, but keep it up. I feel like a new woman.*

She made it home with more than enough time to get dinner ready. When her aunt returned from picking up Meg at day camp, the table was set and the burrito fixings were lined up and waiting for them.

"So, what did you do today?" Aunt Sarah asked as they sat down to eat.

"Oh, nothing," Annie said casually. "This guy asked me out, but it's not a big deal."

"Oh," her aunt answered, reaching for the guacamole. Then she stopped, the spoon piled with avocado and tomatoes in her hand. "Did you say a boy asked you out?" she said.

"Mmm hmmm," Annie said.

Her aunt looked at Meg, who was looking at Annie in amazement. "Meg, did your sister just tell us that she's going on a date?" she said seriously.

"I think so," Meg replied. "With a *boy*. Ick."

Aunt Sarah looked at Annie, an excited smile on her face. "So, tell me *everything*."

Annie told her about Brian and about how she'd played it cool with him. Her aunt listened, spellbound, until her niece was done with her story.

"I don't know what to say," she said. "I'm really proud of you."

"Thanks," said Annie. "I'm pretty proud of me, too."

"But it's with a *boy*," Meg repeated.

Annie and her aunt laughed. "Someday you might think boys aren't so bad," Aunt Sarah said. "Annie used to say the same thing when she was your age."

Meg frowned. "I'm never going to like boys," she said.

"You might change your mind about that," Annie told her little sister. "I did."

"Just like you changed your hair and your clothes?" said Meg.

"Yes," Annie said. "Just like that."

"Just don't change *too* much," Meg said. "I liked the way you were."

Yes, Annie thought as she ate, *but Brian likes the new me. And so do I.*

CHAPTER 8

"So then the judge signed the papers and it was all over." Sasha took a bite of pizza and chewed while Annie, Cooper, and Kate all applauded.

"Now Thea is officially your guardian," Cooper said. "No more jumping from place to place."

"Not if I have anything to say about it," Sasha agreed. "This place is home, and you guys are officially stuck with me."

It was Saturday night, and the girls had gathered for dinner before going to a movie. Sasha was telling them all about her final court date the day before, when a judge had declared Thea, the coven member Sasha had been living with since running away from her previous foster home, Sasha's legal guardian. It had been a long process, and very emotionally draining for Sasha. But now it was over and they were celebrating.

"I know you're all excited for me," Sasha said. "But shouldn't you be spending Saturday night with your boyfriends?"

"I told Tyler that Saturdays are girls' nights out," Kate said. "Besides, I'm seeing him tomorrow anyway."

"Coop?" Sasha queried, employing the nickname only she was allowed to use for her friend.

Cooper swallowed the cheese in her mouth. "T.J. and I are having a little time-out," she said.

"You didn't break up, did you?" asked Sasha, her voice filled with concern. "I like that boy."

"No," Cooper said. "We didn't break up. We're just having a minor disagreement about his well-meaning but freakish desire to censor my work, and my unflinching dedication to honesty and self-expression that prevents me from letting him do it."

"He doesn't want her to talk about witch stuff in her performance pieces," Kate translated for the others.

"That's ridiculous," Annie said instantly.

They all turned to her. She'd been oddly quiet all night, and Cooper was wondering if she was still in the bad mood she'd been in the night of her performance a week before. She hadn't even really responded when Cooper told her how great she looked, and she'd been acting a little weird since they'd sat down.

"No guy should tell you what to do," Annie continued. "It's your life. I hate it when guys think they have to be the big protectors. Thank Goddess Brian isn't like that."

"Brian?" Sasha said. "Who's Brian?"

Annie smiled like she'd been dying for some-one to ask her that question. "Just the guy I went out with last night," she answered.

Sasha, Cooper, and Kate all looked at one another wide-eyed. Cooper put down her slice of pizza and wiped her mouth. "Did you just say 'the guy I went out with last night'?" she asked.

Annie nodded. "That would be correct," she said.

"You went on a date and you didn't tell us?" Kate shrieked. "Annie!"

"I would have told you, but I know you've been busy helping your mom and Cooper's been busy writing, and I didn't want you guys to make a big deal out of it," she said. "It wasn't like it was my first date or anything."

"Yes, it was!" Cooper said.

Annie blushed. "Okay, so it was my first date."

"I can't believe you've kept quiet this long," Sasha said. "Here I've been blabbing about my court thing and you went on an actual date with an actual boy. Spill it, sister."

Annie sat up. "Well," she said. "It was really nice. We met at Grendel's. He brought me a rose."

"Awwwwww," Cooper said, enjoying seeing the blush that crept across Annie's cheeks.

"He brought me a rose," Annie continued. "Then we ate. He had steak or something and I had the shrimp."

"We don't care what you *ate*," Kate said. "Tell us

about *him*. Where did you meet him? What does he look like? Tell us the good stuff."

Annie told them about going into the store and talking to Brian. They all listened raptly as she replayed their conversation. When she described what Brian looked like, Sasha whistled.

"Sounds like a keeper to me," she said.

"Okay," Kate said. "So now we know what he looks like, how he asked you out, and what you had for dinner. That just leaves one more big question."

"Did you kiss him?" asked Sasha, beating Kate to the punch.

"No!" Annie said. "It was just our first date."

Her friends hooted with laughter while Annie blushed some more.

"Good for you," Cooper told her when they'd finished laughing. "That way he'll be sure to ask you out again, just to see if you'll let him kiss you on the second date."

"He already did ask me out," said Annie. "I'm seeing him on Monday."

"I must say, I'm impressed," Sasha told Annie. "Are you sure you're the same girl who wouldn't even talk to the guys on Skip Day a few months ago?"

"Yeah," Kate said. "I'm not sure the rest of us can keep up with you if you keep changing this much."

"Why does everyone keep talking about how much I'm changing?" Annie said. "I'm still me. I just look a little different."

Cooper gave her a look. "And act different and sound different. Annie, you would *never* have talked to a guy before whatever it is that's happened to you happened."

"Nothing has happened!" Annie insisted. "I just got tired of always being boring little Annie."

"You were never boring," Kate said. "Just a little frumpy."

As they were laughing some more Jessica appeared at their table. When she saw her, Annie instinctively grabbed some napkins. They'd deliberately sat at a table outside of her service area to avoid a repeat of the previous Saturday's disaster.

"Don't worry," Jessica said. "I'm Coke-free tonight. I just wanted to stop by and tell you way to go for how you handled Sherrie the other day."

"Sherrie?" Kate said. "You didn't tell us you saw Sherrie."

"See her?" Jessica said. "She *slapped* her. Right in the middle of Banana Republic. I've never seen Sherrie so surprised in my life. I'd give anything to have it on video. Sherrie was so mad she went home and hasn't come out since. I don't think we'll see her until the first day of school. That is, if she doesn't transfer to avoid the humiliation."

"You slapped Sherrie Adams?" Cooper asked, not believing what she was hearing. "As in with your hand?"

"Right across the face," Jessica told them as if she were an announcer doing a play-by-play. "I almost peed myself, it was so good."

Someone at one of Jessica's tables called out to her and she left. When she was gone there was dead silence as Sasha, Cooper, and Kate just stared at Annie.

"What?" Annie said. "So I slapped Sherrie. She had it coming."

"No kidding she had it coming," said Cooper. "But what made you do it?"

"I was just tired of her attitude," said Annie.

"I'm speechless," Kate said. "Absolutely speech-less."

"Well, clearly not absolutely," joked Sasha. "But I'm pretty surprised myself. Annie, you amaze me. I think this deserves hot fudge sundaes all around. What do you say, girls?"

"I'm trying to resist the urge to break into 'Ding! Dong! The Witch Is Dead,'" Cooper said.

"First you have a date and then you slap Sherrie," Kate said. "What next? Are you going to tell us that between this morning and now you found a cure for the common cold?"

"Actually, I slapped Sherrie before I met Brian," Annie said. "I guess I forgot about that in all the excitement about the date thing."

Cooper sat back, looking at her friend. She'd always known that Annie had a fighting spirit in her. After all, it had been Annie's tenacity that had first gotten Cooper to talk to her and Kate about her own interest in Wicca. But she'd never seen Annie use the strength inside her for her own needs, and she was happy to see her doing it now. No matter what Annie said, she *had* changed—for the better.

"We can talk about me later," Annie said. "Let's get back to Cooper. What's this about T.J. trying to censor you?"

"He's afraid that if I talk too much about the whole witch thing that someone is bound to get upset and cause trouble," Cooper replied.

"Why would he think that?" asked Sasha. "Just because they burned millions of witches in the Burning Times doesn't mean they'll do it again now."

"It wasn't millions it was thousands," Kate corrected her. "Remember, I'm the one who did the report on it. And I'm not so sure they wouldn't do it again now."

"Kate doesn't think I should use that material either," Cooper told the others.

"I just think you should be careful," said Kate. "Trust me, people don't like things that they don't understand."

"Are your parents giving you a hard time again?" Annie asked her.

"Not yet," Kate said. "But they're getting more suspicious. No offense, but your performance at lunch the other day didn't exactly help anything."

"My performance?" Annie said. "What are you talking about?"

"I wasn't going to bring it up," Kate said. "But my mom was a little put off by you."

"What did I do?" Annie asked, sounding hurt.

"Never mind your comments about her age and weight," Kate said. "She just thought you were a little—" She paused.

"A little what?" Annie prodded.

"A little out of control," Kate finished. "Actually, she thinks you and Cooper are both kind of on the wild side. I think she's afraid you're rubbing off on me or something."

Annie looked at Cooper, then back at Kate. "Meaning what exactly?" she asked.

"She thinks you guys are a bad influence," Kate said. "And Annie, it didn't help that you almost told her about the Wicca class at lunch."

"That was an accident!" Annie said. "I didn't actually say anything about it, and it wouldn't be a problem anyway if you'd just tell her about it and get it over with."

"You know I can't do that," argued Kate. "There's no way she'd understand that. And then the way you were talking about Tyler, and all of that. It just made her suspicious."

Kate finished and looked down at the table. Neither she nor Annie said anything else. Finally, Cooper spoke.

"We know your situation with your parents is tricky," Cooper told Kate. "But telling your mom that it's just Annie and I who go to the class doesn't make it easy for us either."

"I know," Kate said. "I didn't mean to sound like

I was accusing you guys of anything. I was just trying to say that not everyone is accepting of witchcraft and that sometimes you have to be careful what you say."

"I think you made that point loud and clear," said Annie. "I'm sorry if your mother doesn't like us, but that still doesn't mean Cooper should have to censor her art."

"I didn't say my mother doesn't like you," said Kate.

"Yeah, you sort of did," Cooper said. "Look, Kate, this has been a problem since the very beginning. You've always had to be careful when it comes to your parents' knowing about the witch stuff. Annie and I know that. We didn't even mind when you told your parents that we were into it and you weren't. That wasn't a big deal. But I for one don't want your mom thinking I'm some kind of freak because you're afraid to tell her the truth."

"I'm sorry if I did anything to make her think that I'm wild," Annie added. "But Cooper's right. It's really hard to look normal when she doesn't even know what we're really doing or who we really are. We always have to be careful around her, and that's not easy. It would be a lot easier if you'd stick up for us."

"I do stick up for you guys," Kate said plaintively. "It's not like I don't."

"But you can never really stick up for us until you tell your parents—or at least your mother—what *you're* doing," said Cooper.

Kate looked at Cooper with a pained expression. "I can't," she said. "Not now. Maybe once this whole wedding thing is over. But not right now, I can't."

"We're not asking you to do it now," Cooper told her. "We're just asking you to start thinking about it."

"Okay," Kate said. "I will. I promise."

The four of them sat in silence for a while until Sasha said brightly, "Hey, this is starting to turn into a downer. I say we get things going again with those sundaes. All in favor?"

Cooper put her hand up immediately. Kate followed a moment later. Sasha's was already up. The three of them looked at Annie, who still looked somewhat put out.

"Oh, fine," she said, raising her hand. "There's nothing hot fudge can't fix."

After their desserts the girls walked over to the movie theater and bought tickets. They arrived just as the trailers were starting, and as they sat in the darkness watching previews of the new Julia Roberts movie and the latest from George Clooney, Cooper found herself thinking about T.J. What was he doing? she wondered. They hadn't really talked much since their blowup on Monday, and she wasn't sure where things stood. She'd decided to give her boyfriend a little space, and he seemed to be doing the same for her.

But it's been almost a week, she thought. *He must have gotten over it by now.* She decided to call him when she got home and make nice. She really did want him to be at her performance, and she figured calling would be a nice gesture on her part.

After the film, Kate, Cooper, and Annie said good-bye to Sasha, who lived at the other end of town. Then the three of them got on the bus and rode back to their neighborhood.

"I'm sorry we sort of had a fight tonight," Kate said when they were about halfway there.

"It wasn't a fight," Annie told her. "It was more like excessive tension, and it's okay."

"I really am working on telling her, you know," Kate said.

"Well, keep trying," Cooper remarked. "It gets worse the longer you wait."

As the bus reached their stops they got off and went their separate ways. Cooper walked home, said hello to her parents, and then went to her room. It was time to call T.J. He picked up on the third ring.

"Hey," Cooper said. "How's it going?"

"Okay," T.J. said. He sounded glad to hear from her, which made her feel good.

"I'm sorry about our little blowup the other day," Cooper told him, sounding like Kate half an hour earlier.

"It's okay," said T.J. "We were just saying what we felt."

"So, I'd really like you to come to my perform-ance," Cooper told him. "How about it?"

"I don't know," replied T.J.

Cooper felt her heart sink. "What do you mean?" she asked.

"I'm just not sure I want to be there right now," T.J. told her.

"But I want you there," Cooper said. "I want you to hear me perform."

"I know you do," said T.J. "But I don't think we can agree on this. Not right now anyway."

"So you're never coming to hear me?" Cooper asked angrily.

"I didn't say that," T.J. said. "I just said I'm not sure this is the time for me to be there."

"This is my first big show," Cooper said. "It means a lot to me. I can't believe you won't come."

T.J. sighed. "Let's talk about this later," he said. "It's late and we both probably need to think things through some more before we can really talk."

Cooper wanted to slam the phone down. How could T.J. do this to her, especially after she'd made the gesture of apologizing? He'd had almost a week to think things through. Why did he need more time? She felt as if everything she'd ever thought about him had turned out to be wrong. If he couldn't even support her in this, how could she count on him for anything else?

"Yeah," she said before hanging up. "I think I do have some thinking to do. I'll let you know what I decide."

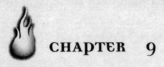

CHAPTER 9

"It feels like I haven't seen you in forever," Tyler told Kate as they walked through the museum on Sunday afternoon. It was a weekend, but the museum wasn't crowded; there were only a few other people wandering the halls besides the two of them. Outside, the sun was shining brightly, and most people seemed to have chosen to be out enjoying the nice weather. Even the security guards seemed to have been lulled into a state of sleepiness by the gorgeous day, and they didn't, as they usually did, eye Kate and Tyler, waiting for them to touch the paintings or make too much noise.

Kate stopped in front of a portrait of a woman holding a small black-and-white dog. "Well, you've been working a lot with Thatcher and I've been working a lot with my mother," she told her boyfriend. "There hasn't been a lot of time for us to do anything."

"The coven didn't even do a Lammas ritual this year because everyone has been so busy," said Tyler.

"We're going to wait until everyone is back."

"I totally forgot about Lammas," said Kate.

Tyler laughed. "A lot of people do," he said. "It's a harvest festival, and now that most of us don't have to worry about threshing wheat and bringing in the corn we tend to not be as aware of that one as we are of some of the others. But it's still important to celebrate it as part of the Wheel of the Year. We'll just do it a little later this year than we usually do."

"When was it?" Kate asked.

"The first of August," said Tyler.

Kate thought for a moment. "That was last Monday," she said. "Right after the blue moon. I wonder if that's why Annie has been acting so weird. Maybe she was mad that first we couldn't do the full moon ritual and then we forgot about Lammas. Not that she mentioned it or anything."

"Annie's been acting weird?" asked Tyler.

Kate sighed. "Remember how she ran out of the restaurant the night of Cooper's reading?"

Tyler nodded. "I thought she was just mad about the Coke thing," he said.

"That's what we thought at first, too," Kate replied. "But it's gotten stranger. It's like she's become this totally different person. First she slapped Sherrie. Then she got this boyfriend."

"Annie has a *boyfriend*?" said Tyler, clearly taken aback.

"Yes," Kate said. "I mean, we're all happy for her

and everything, but it's just sort of weird that it happened so suddenly."

Tyler was chuckling. "Annie has a boyfriend," he kept repeating. "Imagine that."

"First Cooper and now Annie," Tyler said. "I think you started a chain reaction."

"Well, we're not exactly sure Cooper and T.J. are still an item," Kate informed him.

"Why?" asked Tyler. "What happened?"

Kate moved on to another painting—one of a cow standing near a stream—and looked at it for a moment before answering. "They had a disagreement over just how public Cooper should be about being involved in the Craft," she said.

"I thought T.J. was okay with her studying Wicca," said Tyler.

"He is," Kate answered. "He just thinks she should tone it down when she's doing public performances and stuff."

She waited for Tyler's response. The truth was that she'd been trying to find a way to bring up the current subject all day. It was something she needed to discuss with her boyfriend, but she was nervous about it.

"Tone it down?" Tyler repeated. "How so?"

"Well, Cooper wants to do some pieces about her experiences with Wicca," Kate explained. "T.J. doesn't think she should because she might get negative reactions to them."

"Well, she probably will," Tyler said. "But that

doesn't mean she shouldn't do it. Look at my dad. He can't stand anything to do with witchcraft. But my sister and I don't keep quiet about it just because it might upset him."

"Yes, but you and Hannah have a mother who's a witch," Kate reminded him. "You grew up with all of this and you're used to it. A lot of people aren't. Cooper has already had some run-ins with people because she's talked about this stuff."

"You're talking about it like it's something to be afraid of," said Tyler. "Or something to be ashamed of. Yes, there are a lot of people who don't understand what Wicca is all about, but if we all keep quiet about it they never *will* understand it."

Kate wasn't sure what to say next. She and Tyler had very different perspectives on this issue. So far it hadn't really been a big problem, but she'd known for a while that the time was coming when they would have to discuss it. And that time seemed to be now.

"It's not that easy for some of us," she said carefully. "I agree with you that people need to talk about Wicca before they can understand it. But for some people that's really hard."

"You mean like T.J.," said Tyler. "He's afraid of what people will think if Cooper is too vocal about the fact that she's studying witchcraft. I get that. But it's not his life. She has to make those decisions for herself."

"I wasn't talking about T.J.," Kate told him.

"I was talking about me."

Tyler looked at her. "What do you mean?" he asked.

Kate sat down on a bench that was positioned in front of a large abstract painting. Tyler sat next to her, looking into her face with some concern.

"You know my parents are pretty conservative," Kate began. "And you know I don't talk to them about any of this."

Tyler shrugged. "Sure," he said. "I know you have to be a little careful. But that's different. Cooper's parents already know."

"Right," said Kate. "But let's get back to me for a minute. Remember when we did the healing ritual for Aunt Netty and I asked you not to come because I didn't want to have to explain your being there to my parents?"

Tyler nodded. "I didn't like it," he said. "But I didn't want to create any tension during the ritual."

Kate looked at the painting, letting her mind focus on the blobs of blue and yellow paint while she organized her thoughts. She didn't want what she had to say to come out wrong.

"After the ritual my parents wanted to know how involved Annie and Cooper are with the group," Kate said. She paused again, knowing that Tyler wasn't going to like what came next. "And I told them that they were involved but that I didn't really know anything about it."

Tyler didn't say anything, so Kate continued.

"They think that Cooper and Annie are into something they wouldn't like," she said. "And they basically told me to be careful when it comes to being friends with them."

"And what do Annie and Cooper think about this?" asked Tyler.

"They think I need to tell my parents about being in the study group," Kate answered.

"So do I," said Tyler.

"I know you do," Kate replied. "And I *want* to tell them. But I'm scared to do that. I don't know what they'll say. If they tell me that I can't go anymore then I'll lose one of the most important things in my life. At least this way I still have it."

"Yes," said Tyler. "But this way you're always afraid that they're going to find out."

"It's not just the class," Kate continued. "It's you."

"Me?" Tyler said.

"If they know that you're a witch do you really think they're going to want me to see you?" Kate said.

Tyler looked at the floor and didn't say anything.

"Now you see why it can be a big deal," said Kate. "Now you understand why I didn't want you at the ritual and why I don't have you come over a lot."

Tyler looked up. "You mean you've *deliberately* been keeping me away from your parents?" he asked. "I understand about the ritual, but is that why I never come over?"

Kate nodded. "I just don't need them asking a

lot of questions. Especially right now, while they're worried about what I might be doing."

"So what are you saying?" Tyler asked her. "Are you saying you don't want me coming around?"

"I'm saying I'd appreciate it if you could keep a low profile until I can sort all of this out," replied Kate.

"How much lower profile can I get?" Tyler said, sounding annoyed. "I almost never come over. I hardly see you. Do you even tell them that we're going out together?"

"Most of the time," answered Kate.

"*Most* of the time?" Tyler repeated.

"Look," Kate said. "As it is I have to lie to them about where I'm going when I go to class every Tuesday night. Usually I tell them I'm seeing you. I can't be seeing you every time I go out, so sometimes I have to make up stuff."

"Great," said Tyler. "That's just great. You have to lie about going out with me."

Kate sighed. The conversation wasn't going at all the way she'd hoped it would. She'd expected Tyler to understand, even though she knew what she was telling him was difficult to hear. He'd always been so supportive of her. But now he was acting like a typical guy, and she was shocked.

"I'm not exactly lying about you," she said, trying again. "I just can't tell them everything. Not while they're breathing down my neck about Cooper and Annie."

"So when *are* you going to tell them?" Tyler asked her.

Kate looked into his eyes. "I don't know," she said. "I have to think about it."

"You can think about it all you want to," Tyler said. "But eventually you're just going to have to sit down and tell them that you're studying Wicca and your boyfriend is a witch."

He was speaking rather loudly, and at the words "Wicca" and "witch" several people turned around to look at them. Kate noticed a security guard look over toward the bench.

"Could you keep it down a little?" she asked.

"Oh, so now you're afraid of what people in the *museum* think?" said Tyler. "You don't even know them!"

Kate looked at him, hurt. "I don't get it," she said. "I'm trying to tell you how I feel about this."

"No," Tyler said. "You're making excuses about how you feel. Kate, I know what your family is like. I know that Wicca is something they'll have a hard time with. But do you think you're the only one who has ever had to worry about telling people something they don't want to hear?"

"You and Cooper just don't get it," Kate responded. "It's not always that simple."

Tyler took her hand and held it tightly. "I don't want to fight about this," he said. "But I think we have to have this out. What are you going to do, Kate? Are you going to wait until the perfect time? When will that be? When you're in college? When you're twenty-one? When you're not living with them anymore? There's never going to be a perfect time."

"But there *will* be a time when things aren't so stressful," Kate answered. "My mother is worried about the wedding and my aunt, and—"

"There's always going to be something she's worried about," Tyler said. "Always. And as long as you use those things as excuses you will never tell her about yourself. Or about us."

"She knows about us," Kate said weakly.

Tyler shook his head. "Not really," he said. "What do your parents know about me? They know that I go to a different school and that I don't play team sports. That's about it. What did they know about Scott?"

Kate didn't answer for a moment. She knew what Tyler was getting at. And it was true—her parents *had* known a lot more about her old boyfriend than they did about Tyler. He'd often come over for dinner, and they'd even met his parents a few times. Tyler had only been over for dinner once, and she'd never even mentioned Rowan to them. In fact, when Tyler and his family came up in conversation she usually managed to change the subject as quickly as possible.

"I get what you're saying," Kate said softly. "And I know it hurts you that I haven't told my parents everything. But you know I love you."

"I know you do," said Tyler. "And I love you,

too. But I feel like what we have here can't really go anywhere as long as you keep hiding it from your family. And it's not just about us."

"What do you mean?" Kate asked.

"You can't fully develop as a witch if you have to hide what you're doing," he said. "There's always going to be a part of you that isn't involved in what you're studying or doing. Look at what's happening right now—you're having to put all the pressure on your friends because you're afraid of telling your parents that you really are involved just as much as they are. All of us have to be on the lookout because of you."

"Are you telling me that if I don't tell them I should quit studying Wicca?" Kate asked.

Tyler shook his head. "No, that's not what I'm saying," he replied. "But I'm saying that you have to take a good look at how effective what you're learning can be if you always have this pressure of being afraid that someone will find out about you. And you also have to look at how it affects the people around you. Right now you're letting your parents think things about Cooper and Annie that aren't true. And in a way you're letting them think things about me—and about us—that aren't true."

Kate let go of his hand and held hers in her lap. She'd wanted him to tell her that everything was okay and that he understood and would stand by her while she decided what to do. But now she felt as if Tyler was putting her in a position of choosing:

Wicca or her family, him or her family, Cooper and Annie or her family.

"I don't know how to tell them," she said. "I just don't know how. This isn't something they'll understand. I know that."

"I can't tell you how to do it," Tyler said. "If you recall, *I* told my father while we were driving to Christmas Eve services at his church. That probably wasn't the best method. You'll have to decide for yourself how to do it. But I can tell you that the longer you wait the harder it's going to be. Eventually something will happen and you'll be forced to tell them. I can almost guarantee that. Then they'll be upset that you hid it from them. But if you tell them about it on your own terms, that will make things a little easier."

"And what if they tell me I can't go to class anymore?" asked Kate.

Tyler took a deep breath. "I can't tell you that either. You'll have to cross that bridge when you come to it."

"And if they tell me I can't see *you* anymore?" Kate said.

"Can we talk about something that isn't depressing?" asked Tyler.

"Only if you can think of something," said Kate. "Right now I feel like everyone is trying to force me to do something I'm not sure I can do."

"Sort of like the way you're asking us to cover for you?" Tyler responded.

Kate looked away. She knew he was right. She felt as though the time was coming—and soon—when everything was going to blow up unless she made a choice. She'd been telling herself that it would all work itself out, but now it looked as if that wasn't going to happen unless she did something. She just didn't know how—or if—she could do it.

"Look," Tyler said, "I know that this really isn't what you want to hear, but I don't want you lying to your parents about me."

"Meaning what?" Kate asked, turning to look into his beautiful golden eyes. Usually his eyes shone with happiness, but now they seemed clouded over, dulled by worry.

"I don't think we should see each other unless you're going to tell them we're seeing each other," he said. "I don't want you telling them that you're going to the library or to see some other friend or anything. That makes me feel bad, like we're doing something we're not supposed to be doing."

"But it's not like they don't know we're dating," Kate protested. "They know that."

"I understand," said Tyler. "But I don't want to be a secret you have to keep, even if I'm just a part-time secret. I want your parents to know who I am, Kate. I'd like to be able to come over and feel comfortable there. Right now I don't. And now that I know you don't always tell them when we see each other, I'll worry that someone you don't want to see us together will see us. I don't want to see you under those circumstances."

"Are you breaking up with me?" Kate asked, a terrible feeling growing in her chest.

"No," Tyler said. "You're not getting rid of me that easily. But I think we should cool things off until you sort out what you want to do about all of this."

Kate sat on the bench, wanting to cry. She'd begun the conversation wondering how she was going to tell Tyler that he had to keep a lower profile for a while. But now *he* was telling her that he wanted to do the same thing, but for an entirely different reason. *Is this how he felt about what I was asking him to do?* she wondered. If so, it hurt horribly. She felt deeply ashamed that she might have made her boyfriend feel the way she was feeling right then. Was this how Cooper and Annie felt when she pretended to not know anything about what they were all doing?

"I feel really awful right now," she told Tyler.

He put his arm around her and hugged her close while he kissed her on the cheek. "Welcome to your next big challenge," he said.

CHAPTER 10

"What are they doing?" Annie asked Mrs. Abercrombie as she watched some workmen taking things out of Ben Rowe's old room while two other men carried things in.

"There's a new guest coming," the nurse told her.

"A new guest?" Annie said. "Why?"

The nurse smiled. "We can't just leave the rooms empty," she said. "There are a lot of people who need to live here."

Annie relaxed. "I know," she said. "I guess I just thought that it would always be Ben's room. So who's coming?"

Mrs. Abercrombie looked at her list. "Miss Eulalie Parsons," she told Annie.

"Eulalie Parsons?" Annie said. "What kind of name is that?"

"It's a Southern name, young lady."

Annie turned around and saw an old woman standing behind her. She was short—only about up to Annie's chest—and very, very thin. Her curly white hair was gathered into a small knot at the nape of her neck, and she peered at Annie through small round spectacles, her chocolate-colored eyes magnified by the thick lenses so that they appeared to be much larger than they were. She wore a light blue dress the color of the summer sky, and around her neck she wore a beautiful necklace containing a large sapphire.

"Oh," Annie said, startled at the power in the old woman's voice. "I'm sorry. I didn't mean to offend you."

"You didn't offend me," said Eulalie. "Not yet anyway."

"You'll have to excuse my aunt," said a tall woman standing beside the old lady. "She's a little nervous about moving in."

"I'm not nervous at all," Miss Parsons said. "I'm looking forward to it."

"Well, I'm sure Annie will be happy to help you get settled while your niece and I go over the final paperwork," Mrs. Abercrombie said.

"Sure," said Annie. "I'd be happy to."

"Come on then," Eulalie said to Annie as she walked toward her room. "I want to make sure those big lunks carrying my things in don't drop anything."

Annie followed the old woman into what used to be Ben Rowe's room. Eulalie stopped and looked around.

"I like this color," she said, eyeing the blue walls.

"Ben and I painted the room this color," Annie said.

"Ben?" Miss Parsons asked.

"The man who used to live here," explained Annie.

Eulalie nodded. "You and he were friends?"

"Yes," said Annie. "He meant a lot to me."

The old woman nodded but didn't say anything. She went to the window, opened the curtains, and looked outside. "Very nice," she said. "If I have to be locked away it might as well be someplace pretty."

"Don't you want to be here?" Annie asked.

Miss Parsons turned around and fixed Annie with a look. "Nobody wants to be here, do they?" she asked. "Isn't this where they put people when they want to forget about them?"

Annie didn't know what to say. She'd often thought that same thing, but she'd never said it out loud, at least not to any of the residents.

"Oh, don't take me too seriously," Eulalie said, waving at Annie. "I'm sure it will be fine. At least I won't have a great big house to clean anymore."

She walked to the dresser and pulled open the top drawer, examining it as if to see if everything she wanted to put into it would fit. Then she shut it and looked in the mirror that hung behind the dresser. Annie, standing behind her, was reflected in it. Miss Parsons looked closely at the reflection, wiped her hand across the surface of the mirror as if wiping something away, and then turned to peer at Annie with a strange expression on her weathered face.

"You're touched," she said gently.

"Excuse me?" Annie said, not understanding what Eulalie had said.

"Touched," she repeated. She walked closer to Annie and looked at her face. "I saw it in the mirror just now. Can't see it directly, you know. But sometimes in reflections it shows up."

"I don't know what you mean," Annie told her, feeling slightly nervous.

Miss Parsons laughed. "I think you do, girl," she said. "We just probably use different words for it. Touched is what my grandmother would have said. What I mean is, you've got the powers. Do you know what I'm saying?"

Annie smiled. "Yes," she said. "I think I do."

"Folks have different words for it, of course," Eulalie continued. "The shining. Witchcraft. Being blessed. Voodoo. Doesn't matter what you call it, it's pretty much the same. 'Course, what you *do* with it differs from person to person. I myself never went in for any of that dark stuff."

"You have powers, too?" asked Annie excitedly.

Miss Parsons laughed. "Don't sound so surprised, child. A lot of folks do. I just don't go blabbing it around."

"Are you a witch?" Annie asked.

Eulalie laughed, her voice light as a feather.

"I've been called that," she said. "I don't call myself anything really. Like I said, I can do a thing or two. See spirits mostly, and talk to 'em. Tell what's going to happen sometimes. I used to be pretty good with a healing tonic when I had my own garden. Still could be, I suppose."

"Did you ever belong to a, you know, a group or anything?" Annie pressed.

Miss Parsons sighed. "A few of us used to get together and do a bit of work," she answered, smiling slightly as if she were remembering a wonderful moment. "I haven't done that in some time, though."

"I study with a group of other people," Annie told the old woman.

"Do you now?" Eulalie said.

Annie nodded. "Maybe sometime you'd like to meet them," she said. She couldn't believe that Miss Parsons knew about Wicca, even if that's not what she called it.

"Maybe I would at that," Eulalie replied. "But let me tell you something, child. This power around you right now. It's not all your own, is it?"

Annie didn't understand her for a moment. Then she remembered Freya and the ritual she'd done. "I've been working with one of the goddesses," she told Miss Parsons.

"I thought as much," the old woman said. Then she laughed again, but not unkindly.

"Why is that funny?" Annie asked her.

"I'm not laughing at you, girl," said the old woman. "It's just that you're fair near glowing with whatever it is you're playing with. It must be something powerful."

"It is," Annie said, thinking about all of the changes that had occurred since her ritual.

"Just you be careful," Miss Parsons continued. "Don't let it get *too* powerful, now. You don't know what might happen."

"Oh, I think everything is fine," said Annie.

Just then she heard Mrs. Abercrombie's voice in the hallway. She was coming toward the room, and she had Eulalie's niece with her.

"I think you and I will have a lot to talk about in the days to come," Miss Parsons said to Annie. "But now I get to make my niece feel guilty for leaving her poor old aunt in a place like this."

She smiled broadly and Annie smiled back. She knew that any complaining Eulalie did about Shady Hills was an act. Really, the old woman seemed happy to be there. And Annie was happy to have her there, especially in Ben's room. If he couldn't be alive, she couldn't imagine anyone more suited to take his place in her life right now than Eulalie Parsons. It had never even occurred to her that any of the old people might be involved in witchcraft or anything like it. She wondered if there were others at Shady Hills. She pictured a group of them holding sabbat rituals in the great room, and she giggled.

"Is everything okay in here?" Mrs. Abercrombie asked as she entered.

"Oh, it's fine," Annie said. "I was just helping Miss Parsons get settled."

"And how *is* everything?" Eulalie's niece asked.

"The bed's hard and the view stinks," Miss Parsons announced as her niece's face fell.

"Well, we'll just have to see what we can do about that," Mrs. Abercrombie said in her most cheerful voice.

Annie looked at Eulalie, who winked at her. *This one is going to be an experience*, Annie thought as she left the room and went back to her duties.

•

Later that evening, Annie was in the bathroom at home. She'd filled the big old clawfoot bathtub with warm water and added some rose-scented oil she'd purchased on the way home from work. The room was filled with pink and white candles and the voice of Sarah Vaughan rippled through the doorway from Annie's bedroom, where she'd put the CD on her stereo.

The bathroom was steamy and relaxing, and Annie sang along with Sarah as she reclined in the tub and let the water roll over her. She was thinking about her upcoming second date with Brian, and about Eulalie. Everything in her life seemed to be going really well all of a sudden. Ever since the ritual she'd done she seemed to be having extraordinarily good luck.

It's not luck, she told herself as she lifted a handful of sweet-smelling water and poured it over her shoulders. *You're just letting the goddess inside you come out.*

That's really what it felt like. It wasn't like she was a different person or anything; it was more like she had let the strong, powerful, beautiful woman inside of her emerge. And Freya had helped her—*was* helping her. Annie knew that. She had asked the goddess to lend her some of her strengths, and she had done so.

But what was it Eulalie had said about not letting the power around her grow too big? What had she meant by that? It wasn't like Annie was doing a spell or anything. She was just working with Freya, asking for her help. How could that grow out of control? Well, she couldn't worry about that now. She had a date to get ready for.

Annie climbed out of the tub and wrapped herself in a big fluffy white towel. Still humming, she went into her room, sat in a chair in front of her mirror, and began putting on makeup. As she applied some color to her cheeks she looked at her reflection. What was it Eulalie had seen that had made her ask Annie all of those questions? Annie put the makeup brush down and stared at her face in the mirror. Had there been some kind of a sign? Did something about her look weird?

She couldn't see anything different about herself. Sure, she looked a little different with makeup on. Well, a lot different. But it was still *her* underneath all of that. And Eulalie didn't even know how she'd looked before, so what had made her take notice?

Annie looked more closely. The mirror seemed to be clouding over. *It's probably the steam from the bathroom*, she thought idly. She reached out and wiped away the film of vapor. As she did she saw herself in the mirror beneath, and she gasped. For a moment her face had been replaced by another one. It was just for a second, but it had definitely been there. She'd been looking not at her familiar features but those of a much more beautiful woman.

Now her own face was reflected in the glass and the steam had disappeared. Had it all been a trick of her imagination? *It must have been*, she thought as she resumed putting on her makeup. Whatever Eulalie had seen, Annie couldn't see it herself. But she could ask the old woman about it the next time she saw her. Right now she had to get ready for her date with Brian.

Two hours later she was standing on the floor of the Junebug. More precisely, she was being thrown up into the air by Brian as the band played a swing number. As she came back down and he caught her in his arms, she said, "I told you this would be fun."

Brian swung her around, and she spun to a stop as the number ended. "Let's get something to drink," he said.

She followed him to the snack bar, where he ordered sodas for them. Then they went to sit at one of the little tables while the band launched into their next number. Annie sat, listening to the music, as she sipped her drink.

"How did you know about this place?" Brian asked.

"I read about it in the paper," said Annie. "Most of the time it's a bar, but one night a week they open it up to everyone and teach swing dance. I thought it would be interesting."

"Well, it sure has been an experience," Brian answered. "I don't think I've ever done anything quite like it."

They'd spent the first part of the evening taking a quick lesson in the basics of swing dancing. At first it had seemed complicated, but after the instructor ran through a few steps with them Annie found that it was actually really easy. Brian was the one with the hard part. He had to dance and think about what step they would do next. But he was a good lead, and he had gotten the hang of it with only a few minor mishaps.

Then the band had started playing and the real dancing had begun. At first Annie had been hesitant to join in. Everyone else seemed to know what they were doing, and she'd been afraid of messing up. But the music was infectious, and soon she'd been dancing right along with everyone else. Before long she'd forgotten that it was only her first time.

"I've never met anyone who was into this kind of music," Brian said. "I was really surprised when you came into the store, and now you've surprised me again."

"I'm just *full* of surprises," Annie remarked.

"You sure are," said Brian. "And I'm really glad I met you."

Annie looked at him sitting across from her. She was having a great time with Brian. She'd sometimes wondered what dating would be like, and she'd always thought that she would be scared and nervous around a guy. But she wasn't nervous around Brian at all. He made her feel good. She didn't worry about what to say or what to do. For some reason it all came naturally to her.

"I'm glad I met you, too," she said. She still couldn't quite believe everything that was happening. She felt a little like Cinderella, waiting for midnight to come and to find herself the same old Annie. A week before she would never have imagined herself swing dancing with a cool guy. Now she was actually doing it.

"Shall we get back out there?" Brian asked her as the band began another number.

Annie got up and Brian led her to the dance floor, holding her hand all the way. Then they began dancing and she felt herself being spun around, the whole time remaining safely in Brian's sure grip. They danced around one another, the music filling Annie up and urging her to move. It was as if some other part of her had been awakened, and she gave in to it. She lost herself in the joy of moving to the sound, of being swept up in the raw excitement of the band and the crowd.

When the number was over Brian hugged her tightly and spun her around. She laughed, closing her eyes as the room turned beneath the bright lights. She'd never felt so carefree. When Brian put her down she opened her eyes. He was looking into hers, and all of a sudden she couldn't move. She just watched as his face came closer to hers and his lips parted.

When he kissed her she stopped breathing. It was so unexpected that she didn't even have time to worry about all of the things she'd always thought she'd worry about during her first kiss. She felt Brian's mouth against hers and his arms around her. But everything else was lost as a feeling of warmth and joy spread throughout her whole body.

She tried to remember everything. This was her first kiss. Not just her first kiss with Brian, but her first kiss *ever*. She wanted to be able to replay it over and over again. But just as she thought she was finding the words to describe it, it was over. Brian pulled away and looked at her again.

"Wow," he said simply.

"Wow?" Annie asked, not sure what he meant.

"Yeah," Brian said, grinning. "Wow."

He leaned forward and kissed her again. This time, as she kissed him back, Annie was determined to remember everything.

CHAPTER 11

Cooper looked out from behind the black curtain that covered the back of the stage. The tables were filling up quickly, and already Big Mouth was crowded with faces. Sam had done a great job of getting the word out, and they were expecting a full house. Everywhere she looked Cooper saw people talking and looking at their programs.

But she didn't see T.J. She scanned the room, hoping to see his face, but so far he wasn't there. Even though they hadn't spoken since she'd hung up on him she'd hoped that maybe he would change his mind and come see her perform. *He knows this is a big deal*, she thought as she continued to look for him. *I can't believe he isn't here.*

She couldn't worry about T.J., though. She needed to focus on her work. She had written three new pieces for the night's performance, and she had been practicing them repeatedly, determined to make them perfect. This was going to be *her* night. Even though there were several other performers on the bill, she wanted people to go away remembering just one name—Cooper Rivers.

A flurry of movement caught her eye, and she noticed that someone was waving at her. It was Annie. She was walking through the crowd toward a table near the front of the stage, and she had someone with her. *That must be Brian*, Cooper thought. She hadn't met Annie's new boyfriend yet. Now she studied him carefully. He was cute, she thought. He had a nice face, and he smiled a lot.

Annie got herself a good one, she mused. And Annie herself looked great. She was dressed in a sleeveless red dress, and her hair fell around her shoulders in long waves. Cooper still couldn't believe the change in her friend. Every time she saw her, Annie seemed to be more confident, more outgoing, and more flirtatious. It was a little weird, but she was glad to see Annie finally coming out of her shell.

She was happy to see Annie, but she was still annoyed at T.J. And she was also disappointed that Kate and Tyler wouldn't be there. Kate still hadn't really explained to her what had happened between her and Tyler, but she said they were cooling things off for a little while. Although Kate said that it was nothing serious, Cooper had detected a note of concern in her friend's voice that made her wonder if Kate was telling her the whole truth.

Annie finds a guy and Kate and I lose the ones we've got, she thought to herself. *Now isn't that ironic, Alanis.*

"Cooper," someone behind her said. "We're starting soon."

Cooper turned around. "Okay," she said to the stage manager. "I'm just checking out the crowd. Looks like a tough one."

The stage manager laughed at Cooper's joke. "I'm sure you'll be fine," she said. "Just remember, you're on last."

Cooper nodded. She was stoked about being the last one to perform. It was like she was the headliner and everyone else was just opening for her. At least that's how she liked to think about it. The truth was that it was probably alphabetical or totally random.

She went back to the waiting area where the other performers were standing and sitting. Some of them were silently rehearsing their pieces while others were sitting, eyes closed, as if they were meditating. Cooper leaned against the wall and began going over her material in her head. She didn't try to remember every word, though, because she knew that would just clutter her mind up. It would all come when it was supposed to.

A few minutes later the stage manager came back to where they were all waiting. "Okay," she said. "You're on. Jackie, you're up first."

They all wished Jackie good luck and then settled in to wait their turns. They could hear her as she did her performance, and they could hear the applause of the crowd. Cooper listened, taking in

Jackie's words as she spoke. She was good, but Cooper knew that she was better. She didn't think that out of vanity but because she knew it was true. She'd been working hard on her stuff, and she'd gotten it to the point where she was really sure of it. She couldn't wait for her turn onstage.

Three other people went before her. Cooper listened to each one, making mental notes about what each of them did that did or didn't work. When only one more person was ahead of her, she started walking around, warming up by getting herself in the right mood.

"Cooper."

Cooper looked up and saw the stage manager waving her toward the curtain.

"One minute," the woman said.

Cooper walked over and stood at the entrance to the stage. She was ready. She watched as Sam, the coordinator, walked up to the microphone.

"All right," Sam said. "Our next performer is one I'm very excited to introduce. I saw her at Cuppa Joe's a week or so ago and was blown away. I think you will be, too. So give a hand for Cooper Rivers."

Cooper walked onstage as the audience clapped politely. She was very aware that only a few of them knew who she was, and it was going to be her job to win them over and prove herself. She had a brief moment of fear thinking about that, but it was immediately replaced by a surge of excitement as she took her place at center stage. She was the final performer, the culmination of the evening. The spotlight surrounded her, and she looked down at her feet, pausing for dramatic effect. After a moment she lifted her eyes, looked straight into the audience, and began.

"There are two of me," she began, her voice ringing through the space. "The one I take outside and the one I let roam free when I'm alone, safe from what you think and what you feel."

She had written the piece after her fight with T.J. It was about him, but it was also about the people who were listening to her, the people T.J. worried about. Now Cooper felt as if she were facing them, telling them how she felt about what they might think of her.

"The me you see when you pass me on the street is the one I dress up to hide her from your fears," she continued. "I don't want you to see her and look away or call her names. I don't want *her* to have to see the ugliness that is your misunderstanding. So I keep her covered, tucked inside my coat or sleeping behind my sunglasses."

She was reaching the part of the piece she liked the most. She stood up straight and tall, looking defiantly out at her listeners. "But when we get home I tear off her disguise and the two of us run around my room," she said, her voice rising. "We hold hands and we spin and spin and spin, making ourselves dizzy with laughter while we laugh at you and at what you don't know. We dance and sing and make noise like the wildest of all the wild things. And when we're done we sleep in one another's arms, dreaming of the day when we can be one person again."

She stopped and listened as the audience broke into applause. *I wonder if they really understood it,* she thought as she composed herself to begin her next piece. She had been deliberately vague about what she was really talking about. She wanted them to wonder for a while, until her third piece really let them have it.

But now it was time for the second piece. Once more she paused a moment before continuing.

"I want to tell you a secret," she said confidently, as if speaking to a trusted friend who was seated in the last row. "There's something you don't know about me. What? Yes, I'm going to tell you."

She stopped a moment and held her finger to her lips, as if she were thinking about something. "Or maybe I won't," she continued. "Maybe I'll make you guess. Can you do that?"

Again she waited, as if the person she was speaking to were talking back. Then she nodded her head. "Okay," she said. "I'll give you some clues. I'm not like everybody else. I know, that's not really a good one. How about this—I can do things most people can't. What kinds of things? I can talk to ghosts. Did you know that about me? I didn't think so. And did you know that I can walk through fire? Yeah, I can."

She was having a great time. The piece was moving along just as she'd rehearsed it, with all the pauses coming at exactly the right times. She wondered if anyone in the audience was putting two and two together, if any of them remembered her as the girl who had spoken with the ghost of a dead girl back in April.

"I can do all kinds of things!" she cried, lifting her arms up. "I can jump into a volcano and not get burned. I can make you fall in love with me, although I wouldn't bother. I can even stop a speeding bullet. Right, just like Superman. Although I don't wear a cape. Well, only when I want to look cool."

"Have you guessed it yet?" she shouted. "Have you figured it out?"

The house was silent as she looked out at them expectantly, as if waiting for an answer. Then she shrugged her shoulders. "Okay," she said. "I'll tell you. I can do all of this because—" She stopped, knowing they were all waiting to hear the end. Then she laughed. "I can do it all because I'm one . . . of . . . them," she finished, saying each of the last three words slowly and deliberately.

This time the applause took some time to get going. She knew people were confused. That's what she wanted. She wanted them to wonder what she was trying to tell them. All that would become clear in her final piece, and she liked knowing that her audience was hoping to find out where she was going with all of this.

She took a deep breath. This was what it all came down to. This was her last piece, and the last piece of the evening. She wanted everyone to hear it and to leave the club talking about it.

"When they burned me the last time," she said, "they tied my hands behind me and lit my skirts on fire. They watched as the fire ripped away my skin like a child opening a present. I think they were hoping to see my soul scuttle out and dig its way back to hell and the devil. I think they were hoping to see something they all secretly dreamed about. But I didn't give them that. Instead all they saw was my body turning to smoke."

She let the image of the burning woman sink in before continuing. "Well, now I'm back, after many years of sleeping and waiting and growing stronger—strong enough to fight. And this time you won't burn me. This time you won't keep me quiet by cutting out my tongue and asking me to name my sisters and brothers before you break my neck. This time I will speak out in a voice so loud it fills the skies like thunder and my words fall like rain."

She closed her eyes, allowing her voice to become her instrument. She played it like a guitar, making it louder and quieter, harder and softer as she spoke.

"I will rise up into the night and fly across the moon like a bird," she said. "My song will become a hurricane calling the names of the ones who rescued me from those flames and brought me back again whole and beautiful: Hecate, Pele, Oya, Diana, Astarte, Demeter, Kali." Cooper intoned each name of a goddess in a firm voice, as if she really were calling them to be with her onstage. Then she said, "And far below me, you will look up and say *my* name: Witch! Witch! Witch!"

She ended the piece with her arms spread wide and her head thrown back. Applause burst forth from the darkness where the audience sat, and she knew that she had done well. They had understood her pieces, and they liked them. Once again she wished that T.J. had been there to hear it, to see how she had successfully used her experiences with witchcraft to come up with something great. But at least Annie was there. Cooper was glad about that.

She looked down at the table where Annie had been sitting, hoping to see her friend applauding her. But Annie's chair was empty. Brian sat there, clapping wildly, but where Annie had been there was only an empty glass, still half filled with soda.

I hope she didn't run off again, Cooper thought, remembering Annie's behavior the last time Cooper had performed. But Brian was still there, which meant that Annie had to be around somewhere. She wouldn't just leave him there. Cooper hoped she'd heard the last piece. But she would have to wait to find out. It was time for her to leave the stage. She took a final bow and retreated into the curtains.

"Great job," the stage manager said as Cooper entered the backstage area.

"Thanks," Cooper said. She looked back out through the curtains as Sam walked up to the microphone. She was still riding high on the success of her performance, and she hoped Sam was happy with what she'd done.

"That young woman is someone to watch, isn't she?" Sam said. The crowd applauded again, and Cooper felt her heart swell with pride. She *had* done well.

"I know the program says that Cooper was the last performer," Sam continued. "But we have one more surprise for you tonight. This afternoon I had a visit from another young woman who asked if she could take part in one of our New Words nights. I was going to wait until next month to feature her, but I was so impressed with what she did that I didn't want to wait to introduce her to you. So if you will, please give a Big Mouth welcome to our final performer—Freya."

"Freya?" Cooper said to the stage manager. "Who's Freya?"

"Beats me," the woman answered. "Sam just told me about her a few minutes ago."

Cooper watched as someone emerged from the curtains at the opposite side of the stage. When she saw who it was her mouth dropped open in shock.

"Annie?" she said.

"Someone you know?" asked the stage manager.

"Well, I thought I did," Cooper replied.

She stared at Annie as she walked to the microphone. What was going on? Why was she calling herself Freya? What was she doing? Annie had never performed anything in her life. But there she was, standing on the stage where only moments before Cooper had been standing. All Cooper could do was watch and wait to see what her friend was up to.

Annie cleared her throat and began speaking. "In the velvet of the morning I see them come, carried in the arms of Valkyries. Stained with blood and covered in the dirt of battle, they have become children, sleeping without dreams."

Annie's voice sounded strange, almost unearthly. Cooper had never heard her speak that way. And she certainly had never heard Annie recite any kind of poetry or performance piece. But there she was, her hand wrapped around the microphone as she spoke.

"I go to them and wipe their brows with my golden hair," she continued. "I sing to them of summer and of love among the flowers."

Who does she think she is? Cooper wondered as she listened to Annie. *This sounds like a bad Stevie Nicks song.*

"When they open their eyes and look at me I know they see the faces of the ones they long to kiss. But when they speak they call not their names but mine. Freya. And then I take them by the hands and lead them into the halls of rest."

Annie finished. Cooper was stunned. Her piece had been really bad, like something written by a lovesick teenage girl after reading too many fairy tales. She hoped that Annie wasn't too embarrassed.

But then she was even more surprised to hear the audience erupt into thunderous applause. What were they thinking? Annie's stuff had been awful. But there they were, clapping like mad for her. It was like she'd cast some bizarre spell over them to make them think it was good.

"Thank you," Annie said, as if she'd just performed some amazing song or something. "Thank you so much."

Cooper watched as her friend left the stage. This time she walked through the curtains on Cooper's side of the stage.

"Hey," Annie said when she saw Cooper. "What did you think?"

Cooper looked at her. Should she say something? She still wasn't sure what had happened. All she knew was that Annie had totally stolen the show. Nobody was going to talk about Cooper's performance. She was sure of that. They were all going to talk about Freya and how good she'd been.

"That was something else," Cooper said. "Really something else."

Annie smiled. "I hope you don't mind me doing it," she said. "I just thought it would be fun. I didn't know Sam would put me on tonight."

Before Cooper could say anything Sam came over to them. "That was beautiful," she said. "I loved how you combined traditional poetry with more modern ideas. I was wondering if you'd like to do another show next month."

"Sure," Annie said. "That would be great."

"I'll put you down, then," Sam said, smiling. "Oh, and Cooper, great work, too. Thanks a lot for coming."

Sam walked away. Cooper stared after her. Wasn't Sam going to ask her to be in another show, too? How could she ask Annie and not her? She had been a billion times better than Annie—or Freya— had been.

She turned to say something to Annie but saw that she was surrounded by a group of people, all of whom were telling her how great she'd been. Annie was smiling and laughing, clearly reveling in the attention.

Cooper turned and walked back to the dressing rooms. She grabbed her bag and headed for the back door. She didn't know what Annie was up to, but she sure wasn't going to wait around to find out.

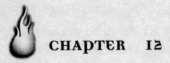

CHAPTER 12

"I'm telling you, it was just like that old Bette Davis movie *All About Eve*," Cooper said to Kate.

"Sorry," Kate answered. "Never saw it."

"Bette Davis plays this actress who takes a young girl she thinks is a fan under her wing. Only the girl turns out to be this scheming wanna-be actress who ends up sabotaging Bette Davis's career and taking over a part meant for her," explained Cooper, sounding very bitter.

"It doesn't sound like Annie did anything quite that bad," said Kate. She was interested in what Cooper was saying, but she was also trying to concentrate on counting how many little paper cups of nuts and candies she'd put together. She was helping make the table favors for the wedding, and she was growing impatient with trying to make sure there were equal numbers of white-chocolate-coated almonds and candied violets in each one. Holding the phone against her shoulder was making it all that much harder.

"Oh, no," Cooper replied sarcastically. "She only stole the show and upstaged me with that weird poem about dead soldiers or whatever it was."

"I'm sure she didn't mean anything by it," said Kate. "I bet she just wanted to feel like she was part of the action."

"And what's with calling herself Freya?" Cooper snapped, ignoring Kate. "Is it supposed to be like Cher or Madonna or Enya or something? I don't get it. Why couldn't she be just plain old Annie?"

"Have you talked to her about this?" Kate asked, sighing. She'd lost count of how many candied violets she'd used, and now she was afraid she was going to run out.

"No," answered Cooper. "I left while she was greeting her adoring fans. I haven't talked to her since then. She called this morning but I had my mother tell her I was out."

"I think you need to talk to her about this and not to me," said Kate. "I don't know why she did it any more than you do."

"I just think something is up," Cooper said. "You said she acted really weird around your mother."

"True," Kate said, adding almonds to some cups that looked bare.

"And there's the whole thing with the look and the attitude and the boyfriend," added Cooper.

"Oh, tell me about the boyfriend," Kate said, suddenly becoming interested again.

"He's okay," Cooper admitted. "I didn't actually talk to him. But he looks nice."

"What does he look like?" Kate asked.

"I don't know," said Cooper. "Tall. Light brownish hair. Two eyes. A nose. He looks like a guy."

Kate groaned. "You are so not helpful sometimes," she said.

"Let's get back to Annie," Cooper replied. "Do you think she's done some kind of a spell? You know, to make herself more popular or something?"

"Annie?" Kate answered. "She wouldn't do that. She knows what would happen if she tried to do a spell like that."

"I know she *knows* what would happen," said Cooper. "But do you think maybe she decided to risk it anyway?"

"That's really doubtful," Kate told her. "But if it makes you feel any better, we can talk to her tonight and ask her in person. We're supposed to meet her at six to go rollerblading. You can come along."

"Rollerblading?" Cooper said. "Since when do you rollerblade?"

"Since when do I not? My dad owns a sporting goods store! Besides, this was Annie's idea," Kate said. "It sounds fun. We're going to the park and Annie's going to rent blades at that place next to it."

"I told you something weird has happened to her," said Cooper.

"Just come with us," Kate told her.

"Okay," Cooper said doubtfully. "But I'll bet

good money she's done something."

"Fine," said Kate. "If she has, then I'll owe you twenty bucks. But my money says that there's a perfectly good explanation for all of this."

"You're on," Cooper told her. "I'll see you tonight, then. We can play good cop, bad cop."

Kate hung up and returned to filling baskets. She'd totally lost count, and now she was just tossing candied violets and nuts randomly into the cups.

"How's it going?" her mother asked as she came into the kitchen with an armload of bags.

"Fine, I think," Kate replied. "I'll just be glad when this is over."

"Tell me about it," said her mother as she set the bags on the counter. "Three days until this wedding, and I still don't have enough people to help serve. Four of the ones I hired called today to say they couldn't make it."

"What do they have to do?" asked Kate.

"Just stand at the tables and make sure all the plates are kept filled," her mother told her. "Oh, and one or two of them will have to walk around with trays of hors d'oeuvres."

"That sounds easy enough," said Kate. "I can do that."

"That still leaves me at least three people short," Mrs. Morgan said. "As if I don't have enough to deal with right now."

"I have a suggestion," said Kate hesitantly.

"What's that?" asked her mother.

"How about if I ask Cooper and Annie to help out?" said Kate.

Her mother paused. Kate knew that she was weighing her reservations about Kate's friends against her need to have people to help out at the wedding. Kate took the opportunity to press her point. "How difficult can it be to carry trays?" she said. "They'll be fine."

"I don't know," her mother said. "This is a *really* big deal for me. It all has to go perfectly."

"I promise they'll be on their best behavior," Kate told her, trying to look as earnest as possible.

Her mother looked back at her for a long time, an expression of uncertainty on her face. "What color is Cooper's hair right now?" she asked. "I can't have a green- or pink- or blue-haired server."

Kate had to think for a minute. "Black," she said.

Mrs. Morgan sighed. "Okay," she said. "But tell them they have to wear black. And nothing too short. Especially Annie."

"Will do," said Kate happily. She was pleased that her mother was letting her and her friends help out. It would give her a chance to see that they really were normal after all. Plus it would show her friends that she wasn't ashamed of them. As she went back to work she congratulated herself on having come up with such a brilliant idea.

Now, if you could just find a way to make Tyler a bigger part of your life you'd be all set, she told herself. It lessened her excitement somewhat to think about that, but it was something she was going to have to deal with, and soon. Ever since their talk at the museum she had been going over and over the conversation in her head. Tyler had been right; he could never fully be her boyfriend until she didn't have to worry about hiding who he was—and who she was—from her family.

They had talked several times since Sunday, but she hadn't seen him again. He had made it clear that while he loved her he couldn't handle having to feel like she was afraid of her family's knowing too much about him. She'd told him that she would do something about that, just as she'd told her friends the same thing. But every time she looked at her mother and thought about beginning a conversation about witchcraft she froze up. She just didn't know how to do it.

Well, this is a start, she told herself as she finished up the last of the favors. If everything went well at the wedding, her mother would be in a good mood and maybe Kate could bring up the subject of her involvement in the Wicca study group. Besides, her mom would be pleased with how well Annie and Cooper behaved, and that would help. She couldn't wait to meet them that evening and tell them the good news.

***

At six o'clock Kate was seated on the bench in front of the rollerblade rental place. She was fastening her blades while Annie removed her shoes and put her rentals on.

"I bet Cooper bails," Annie said as she strapped on a pair of elbow pads. "This is so totally *not* her thing."

"I think she'll be here," Kate said. "She seemed really into it, and I know she wants to see you."

"I don't know why she ran away the other night," said Annie. "Everyone was hoping she'd come to the party afterward."

"I think she needed to get home," Kate said. Was it really possible that Annie didn't know she'd offended Cooper? That seemed unlikely. But she didn't seem at all upset or worried about what had happened at Big Mouth. *I bet Cooper really was blowing it all out of proportion*, Kate thought.

"I can't wait for you to meet Brian," Annie said, continuing to chatter on happily.

"I can't wait to meet him either," Kate replied. "I hear he's cute."

"Did Cooper say that?" asked Annie, smiling. "Well, he is. He's like a cross between Dawson and Mulder."

Kate laughed at how happy Annie sounded. She really was glad to see her friend so excited about life. But she also had to agree with Cooper that it seemed odd that while Annie's life was coming together theirs seemed to be unraveling.

As she was thinking about it she saw someone come flying by on blades, arms waving around before almost colliding with a nearby tree. When the skater finally stopped and turned around Kate saw that it was Cooper, all done up in a helmet and pads.

"I thought I'd get here a little early and get some practice in before you two showed up," Cooper said, clomping over to the bench. "I think I'm getting the hang of it."

She fell, her arms flailing. Kate and Annie reached out and grabbed her before she went over backward. "Or maybe not," Cooper said, righting herself.

"We'll go slow," said Kate.

They skated over to the window, where she and Annie handed the attendant their shoes. Then they began to roll along the paved path that ran through the park. There were a number of other skaters, as well as joggers, dog walkers, and people just hanging out enjoying the beautiful August evening.

"Just take it easy," Kate said to Cooper as they skated. "Don't try to force the skates to do anything or you'll end up on the ground."

"All I want them to do is keep going forward," said Cooper as she narrowly escaped running into a couple who were holding hands.

"So, how are things with T.J.?" Annie asked, gliding along easily. "I didn't see him at Big Mouth the other night."

"He was boycotting," said Cooper. "I haven't

talked to him, so I don't know how he is."

"You two should make up," Annie said, as if she'd given the subject a lot of thought. "You're good for each other."

Cooper snorted. "Tell him that," she said.

"I hear you brought the house down, Annie," Kate said. "Or should I say Freya?"

Annie laughed. "I know that sounds ridiculous," she said. "But I wanted to surprise Cooper, and that was the first name that popped into my head."

"I had no idea you were interested in performance art," Kate remarked, trying to get the conversation headed in the right direction.

"I didn't know either," Annie replied. "It just sort of came to me the day of the show, and I thought I'd see what happened. I think it went really well, don't you, Cooper?"

Cooper didn't say anything for a moment. When she finally spoke she said, "Actually, Annie, I thought it was a little strange."

Kate could see the look of confusion on Annie's face. She knew Cooper was doing her best not to turn the conversation into an argument, but she also knew that Cooper wasn't always the most tactful person in the universe.

"Cooper means we're a little curious about everything that's been happening to you lately."

"What do you mean?" Annie asked.

"Well," Kate said, "we were just wondering if maybe you happened to do anything in particular to induce these changes."

"I don't get it," said Annie.

"Have you done any spells or anything?" Cooper asked bluntly, sounding exasperated.

Annie laughed. "Spells? No, of course not. You know I'd tell you if I did."

"We know," Kate told her. "We're just asking."

"Do you guys think I did some kind of spell to get Brian?" Annie asked. "Because I didn't."

"It's not just Brian," said Cooper, swerving shakily around a rottweiler that was chasing a ball across the path. "It's the new look and the sudden interest in spoken word performances."

"And slapping Sherrie," Kate added. "It all seems to have happened at once, and we were just curious if maybe you'd had a little, you know, magical help."

"I assure you it's all me," Annie said. "I don't really know what happened. I just decided to change the way I look at things, that's all. I thought you guys would be happy for me."

"We are," said Kate. "Really. Aren't we, Cooper?"

When Cooper didn't respond, Kate repeated herself. "Aren't we, Cooper?"

"Right," Cooper said. "Really happy."

"You don't sound happy," said Annie.

Kate paused, unsure of how to continue. "It just seems a little odd, is all," she said finally.

"What?" Annie asked. "Because I've never done anything interesting? Because you're used to my being the boring one? Because you guys are usually the ones who have all the cool stuff happen to you?"

Kate was silent. The truth was that Annie was right. They *were* used to her being the boring one. Well, not boring, exactly, but certainly not like the way she was now. She was the practical one, the one who didn't do outrageous things.

"I'm sorry that you and Tyler are having problems," Annie said. "And, Cooper, I'm sorry that things aren't going well with T.J. and that people liked my piece at the reading more than they liked yours. I can't help those things."

"It's not so much what you're doing as how you're doing it," Cooper said. "You just seem to be enjoying it all a little too much. It's like you're trying to show us up or something."

"I'll try to be more depressed next time something good happens to me," Annie said, sounding angry.

Kate groaned silently. Things weren't going at all the way she had hoped they would. "We're not accusing you of anything," she said.

"Yes you are!" said Annie. "You're acting like I did something wrong and need to be punished."

"We just want to make sure you're not doing anything that might be dangerous," said Cooper. "Remember what happened with the Tarot cards?"

"Yes," said Annie. "I do. Do *you* remember what happened when Kate tried to do a love spell? And do *you* remember what happened when you talked to that reporter, Amanda Barclay? It seems to me the two of you don't have a lot to say about being careful when it comes to magic. So stop lecturing me about it. You don't even know what you're talking about."

Annie speeded up, pulling away from Kate and Cooper.

"Annie!" Kate called. "Come back. That's not what we were saying."

But Annie kept going, rounding a curve and disappearing. She clearly wanted to get away from her friends, and Kate knew that there was no sense in pursuing her. Besides, Cooper was having trouble just staying on her feet. There was no way they were going to be able to catch up with Annie.

Kate stopped, grabbing on to Cooper and slowing her down as well. "Let her go," she said.

Cooper looked at Kate. "I think that went well," she said grimly.

"She has a point, you know," said Kate. "We *have* screwed up a lot more than she has. Maybe we are just a little bit jealous of all the good stuff happening to her."

"Maybe," Cooper admitted. "So what now?"

"I'll talk to her tomorrow and smooth things over," Kate said. "I think she'll take it better coming from me than from you right now. You can talk to her later. Right now let's concentrate on getting you back to the rental place in one piece.

Oh, and I have a question for you."

"What's that?" Cooper asked as they started off again.

"How good are you at balancing a tray on one hand?" Kate asked.

CHAPTER 13

Annie was fuming. How dare Kate and Cooper accuse her of doing something wrong? She couldn't believe it. They were supposed to be her best friends, and best friends were supposed to be *happy* for you when good things happened. They weren't supposed to act like you could only get those things by doing a spell. But that's exactly what they'd said to her.

Why couldn't they accept that she had found a boyfriend and discovered a new side of herself all on her own? Well, not entirely on her own. She knew that a lot of it had to do with the ritual she'd done asking Freya for help. But that wasn't the same thing as doing a spell. Not at all. It was just asking for a little push.

So why hadn't she told them about the ritual, then? That would have been the easy thing to do. They would understand that. They'd have to. They'd all done rituals and meditations designed to help them figure things out or to just focus and energize themselves. This was no different. But she hadn't told them.

And why should I? she asked herself as she snapped open a sheet and smoothed it over Mr. Bryer's bed. If they were going to jump to conclusions that was their problem. She wasn't going to let that stop her from enjoying what was going on in her life. She had Brian. She had her confidence. She had the experience of being onstage and having people listen to her. No one could take those things away. Besides, she deserved them. She'd been the only one who was willing to take time to do a ritual on the blue moon. Cooper and Kate had been too busy. It wasn't her fault that now they were feeling left out.

"You fold those corners any tighter and Mr. Bryer's going to need a shoehorn to get into that bed."

Annie looked and saw Eulalie Parsons standing in the doorway of the room. She was wearing a pale yellow dress that contrasted beautifully with her dark skin and reminded Annie of sunflowers.

"Good morning," she said, happy to see the old woman. "How are you?"

"Oh, just fine," Eulalie replied. "I'm trying to keep away from that nurse. She wants me to have a physical, and I'm in no mood to be poked and prodded today. I keep telling her I'm not a prize melon but she doesn't pay me no mind."

Annie laughed. There was something she'd been

meaning to ask Miss Parsons, and now seemed as good a time as any.

"You know the other day when you said I was sort of glowing?" Annie asked her.

Eulalie nodded and cocked her head. "Sure I do," she said.

"What exactly did you mean?" said Annie.

Eulalie smiled, her bright white teeth flashing. "Well, you know how people talk about guardian angels?" she said.

"Yes," Annie said.

"Well, it's something like that," Miss Parsons explained. "Some people also talk about seeing auras around folks—colors and whatnot. It's kind of like that, too."

"I'm not sure I understand," said Annie.

"We've all got energy around us," Eulalie said. "But there are different kinds of energies. Some of us have spirits who follow us around looking after us. Some of us have all kinds of darkness that hangs over us like rain clouds. And some of us have bright light just radiating out from the inside. We're all different that way. Some of us might have a lot of different things hanging around, or different things at different times."

"And you can see these things?" Annie asked.

Eulalie nodded her head. "Sometimes I can, yes," she said. "Like I told you before, sometimes I see the spirits. Sometimes I just see colors or what have you. Take that nurse Abercrombie. She's got so much white light around her it's like looking into the gates of heaven sometimes. She just wants to help everybody, and it shows. But then you got Mr. Charles down in room 301—he's just sitting there waiting to die. Hurts me to see him in there, all surrounded by grayness and gloom."

"And what did you see when you looked at me?" said Annie.

Miss Parsons smiled. "Around you I saw something special," she said. "You got light there, all right. Pink and white and gold. Like a field of flowers. But you got something else there too. You got someone walking with you, standing behind you and watching out."

"An angel?" asked Annie. "Is that what you mean?"

Eulalie shook her head. "No. This is something else. Not an angel, not a spirit. Can't say I ever saw anything quite like it before. Can't say as I understand it. That's why I told you to be careful with it."

Annie thought about what the woman was saying. Could she really see something around Annie, or was she just talking? She *was* old. It was possible she was a little mixed up. But she seemed so sharp, and what she said about Mrs. Abercrombie and Mr. Charles made sense. *I wonder if she really is seeing Freya,* Annie wondered excitedly. Was the goddess really with her all the time?

"You don't think this thing could hurt me, do you?" she said.

"Not on purpose," said Eulalie. "But even good energy can cause problems when you get too much of it. Whatever this is with you, it likes helping you out. I can see that. But it might try to help you a little too much sometimes. Do you see what I'm saying?"

"I think so," Annie said. "Miss Parsons, when did you start being able to see these things around people?"

"Call me Miss Eulalie, girl," the old woman said. "That's what everybody down home calls me. And to answer your question, I've been seeing things since I was just a little girl. My mama used to see me talking to people who weren't there, and she knew I had the gift. But it wasn't till later that I started understanding who and what I was talking to. As I got older and understood more, the gift got stronger. That's how it works, you know."

"Yes," Annie said. "I do know. But I just started using my gifts, so I have a long way to go."

Miss Parsons laughed. "That you do," she said. "But you're on your way, child. You're on your way. And now I've got to get me out into that garden back there. It's too nice a day to be locked up in here. Besides, I don't think that nurse will think to look for me out behind the azaleas."

She waved at Annie and left. When she was gone, Annie went and stood in front of the mirror over Mr. Bryer's dresser. She peered into it, looking for any trace of the figure Miss Eulalie said she saw around her. Annie knew that the old woman had to be talking about Freya. But was the goddess really with her all the time? She recalled the glimpse of the face she'd seen in her own mirror after her bath. Maybe Freya *was* there. She liked that idea. She liked thinking that she had her very own goddess. It made her feel special.

You are *special*, a voice in her head said.

"You're right," Annie said. "I am."

She smiled at her reflection before going back to work. For the rest of the day she felt really good. She kept thinking about what Miss Eulalie saw when she looked at her, and she imagined Freya standing behind her, enveloping her in her light. *I wonder what will happen next?* she thought as she changed beds, swept floors, and helped Mrs. Abercrombie in the office.

When it was time to go home she decided to go say good night to Miss Eulalie. She felt as if the old woman was becoming a friend, and that made her feel great, too. It was one more good thing that had come her way since doing the ritual.

She walked to the old woman's room. As she neared it she heard the sound of Miss Eulalie's voice. She was talking to somebody. Annie paused outside her door, not wanting to interrupt her visit. But as she listened she realized that while Eulalie was talking, no one was answering her.

"I know you worry about her," Miss Eulalie said softly.

There was a pause, as if she were listening as her companion spoke. Then she said, "You know you can't tell the young ones what to do any more than our parents could have told us."

Who is she talking to? Annie wondered. She peeked inside the door to see if maybe someone really was in the room. But there was Miss Eulalie, sitting on the edge of her bed and looking at the empty air beside her.

Eulalie laughed. "I see why the two of you hit it off," she said. "And yes, I'll tell her. When the time is right I'll let her know you miss her. I think she misses you, too. I can see it in her eyes. She'll be happy to hear from you, I'm sure."

Annie was puzzled. Who was Miss Eulalie talking about, and who was she talking to? *Maybe she's crazy,* Annie thought suddenly. *Maybe everything she's been telling me is just made up.*

"Okay then," Eulalie said. "I'll be talking to you later, Ben. Good-bye."

Ben? Annie thought, hearing what the old woman said. Was Eulalie talking to Ben Rowe? Annie didn't know what to think. Eulalie had said that she could talk to spirits. Was she talking to the ghost of Annie's dead friend? If so, had he really said that he missed her? She wanted to rush in and ask Eulalie if what she'd heard was true. But she didn't want her to think that she'd been spying.

Ben, she thought, suddenly feeling very lonely. *I do miss you.*

She walked away from Miss Eulalie's door. She knew she wouldn't be able to pretend that she hadn't heard anything, so the easiest thing to do was leave. If Eulalie was talking to Ben's spirit, she clearly didn't want Annie to know about it yet. But what had they been discussing? Eulalie had mentioned something about Ben's being worried about her. What had she meant? Why would her old friend be worried about her?

She would ask Miss Eulalie later. There was time. Right now she wanted to get home. She was supposed to meet Brian at the record store later, and they were going to go to a movie. She'd bought a new dress, and she couldn't wait for him to see her in it.

When she got off the bus half an hour later she was surprised to see Kate walking down the sidewalk toward her. Annie was tempted to just keep walking, but Kate waved at her and she stopped.

"Good timing," Kate said. "I was just walking over to your house."

"Why?" asked Annie coldly.

"I want to talk to you," said Kate.

Annie shifted her backpack on her shoulder. "Why, so you can lecture me again?" she asked.

Kate shook her head. "I'm sorry about last night," she said. "So is Cooper. We didn't mean all that to come out the way it did. We were just both a little worried."

"*Were?*" Annie asked.

"You're right," said Kate. "We should have known you wouldn't do anything that was out of line. It's just that you kind of took us by surprise."

"I wanted you guys to be happy for me," Annie told Kate. "I wanted you to be proud of what I've done."

"We are," Kate said. "But you have to admit that you really haven't been acting like yourself."

"Well, this is a new me," Annie said. "I was tired of the old Annie."

"Do you mind if I ask what made you decide to do all of this?" asked Kate.

Annie looked at her friend. Was it time to tell her about the ritual? Did she want Cooper and Kate to know that she had invoked Freya? No, she decided. Not yet. She wanted to keep Freya to herself, at least for a little while longer.

"It was nothing in particular," she said. "Really," she added when she saw Kate looking at her skeptically.

"Well, we're sorry if we hurt your feelings yesterday," said Kate. "We really are happy for you."

"It's okay," Annie replied. "I know I've been having all the luck lately. But don't worry. I'm sure you and Cooper will have your turns, too."

"Maybe," Kate answered. "In the meantime, I have to get home and help my mother wash about a billion pounds of fruit. Which brings me to the other reason I wanted to talk to you. How would you like to make a hundred bucks?"

"Doing what?" Annie asked.

"Helping out at this wedding on Saturday," said Kate. "My mom needs servers. Cooper and I are going to do it. I think I'll ask Sasha, too."

"Well, Brian and I were going to go to the beach," Annie said doubtfully.

"Please?" asked Kate. "I'm really in a bind here. And it will be fun. I hope."

Annie looked at her friend's face. Kate wore a pleading look. Annie sighed. "Okay," she said. "The beach can wait."

Kate beamed. "Thanks," she said. "Be at the museum at nine, and wear something black."

"Nine?" Annie repeated. "On a Saturday?"

"I owe you!" Kate said, pretending to not hear her as she walked away.

Annie turned and walked toward home. *Kate's right*, she thought. *She does owe me. Big time*. Not only was she giving up a date with Brian but she was getting up at an ungodly hour on a weekend to go help someone who thought she was a bad influence on her daughter. At least this was a chance to make another impression on Mrs. Morgan. *And I know just which dress to wear*, Annie thought happily.

CHAPTER 14

"All these secrets. All these lies. Built around my heart. One by one they come undone and all that's left is truth."

Cooper sang the words to the song that was blasting in her ears through the headphones. She was sitting on her bed, trying to write some new material. But she was stuck, so she'd pulled out some tapes of songs she'd written and was listening to them, hoping to get some inspiration. This was one of her favorite songs. She'd written it during the time when she'd been trying to sort out the mystery of Elizabeth Sanger's death. It was a good song. Really good.

But listening to it also made her sad. She'd been playing it for T.J. the night the newspapers had printed the story about her having the visions. When Mouse and Jed, her other bandmates, had come into the garage carrying the paper she'd run out, afraid that they, and especially T.J., would think she was a freak. A few days later, T.J. had given her the tape the band had recorded of the song, and she'd known that it had been his way of saying that everything was okay.

Now, though, it looked like things weren't okay after all. She hadn't talked to T.J. in days. *You're the one who hung up on him*, she reminded herself. *Yeah*, she argued, *but he's the one who was being a jerk in the first place*.

She'd been going over the situation with her apparently now ex-boyfriend in her mind all day. Actually, she'd been thinking about it since the blowup with Annie the night before. Was Annie right? Was she just jealous because Annie had a boyfriend while hers seemed to have disappeared on her? And was she jealous because people had liked Annie's stuff more than they'd liked hers?

Yeah, she thought. *I am*. Mostly because the crowd at Big Mouth had liked Annie's piece, which Cooper still thought was kind of lame. But she was also irritated about the whole boyfriend thing. No, it wasn't Annie's fault that she and T.J. had fought. And she couldn't begrudge her friend the fact that she'd found a great guy. Well, she *shouldn't* begrudge her that. But she was doing it all the same.

The phone rang and Cooper picked it up.

"Hey," Kate said. "I just got through talking to Annie."

"What a coincidence," Cooper said. "I was just thinking about her."

"Everything's cool," said Kate. "She's on for

Saturday. I told her we were sorry we kind of ganged up on her."

"What did she say?" Cooper asked.

"Not much," Kate told her. "She still says she didn't do anything. I guess we have to believe her."

Cooper sniffed. "We don't have much choice," she responded.

"You really don't, though, do you?" asked Kate.

"I don't know what to think about anything right now," admitted Cooper.

"Still no word from T.J.?" asked Kate.

"No," Cooper said.

There was a long pause before Kate said, "At the risk of getting in trouble again for telling my other best friend what to do, I think you should call him."

"But he—" Cooper began.

"I know," said Kate, cutting her off. "He pissed you off. That's what boys do. And maybe he's wrong. But if you want to see him again someone has to make the first move."

"But he—" Cooper said again.

"Do you want to see him?" Kate asked, interrupting.

Cooper hesitated. "I guess I wouldn't mind," she answered.

"Coming from you that's a yes," her friend said. "So call him already."

"I can't do that," said Cooper.

Kate sighed. "Fine," she said. "I'm through telling everyone what to do. You sit there and sulk. I have strawberries to pick over. I'll talk to you later."

She hung up and Cooper put down the phone. She put the headphones on again and turned the song on. But every time she heard it, it just reminded her of T.J., and that made her mad. She didn't want to think about him.

"I will *not* call him," she said out loud. "I will not. He can just call me."

She listened to the song for another half a minute before turning off the stereo and tossing the headphones onto the bed.

"Oh, fine," she said as she stood up and reached for her shoes. "Goddess, I hate being the girl sometimes."

She grabbed her car keys from her dresser and went downstairs before she could convince herself to not do what she was doing. Then she jumped into her Nash Metropolitan convertible, started it up, and took off down the street toward T.J.'s house.

It took her a while to get there, and by the time she pulled up in front of his house she had thought of a million things to say to him. She was trying to decide which one of them to start with when a guy walked out of the garage next to the house. He was wearing a grease-stained white T-shirt and jeans, and he wiped his hands on a rag as he walked toward her. With his short red hair, muscular body, and freckles, he looked like an older, hunkier version of T.J.

"Nice car," he said, eyeing the Nash. "Is it a nineteen fifty-six?"

"Nineteen fifty-seven," Cooper corrected him.

The guy nodded. "I should have known from the amber taillights. Before 'fifty-six they were plain old white."

"I'm assuming you're one of the infamous McAllister boys," Cooper said. "Let me guess— Seamus?"

"Close," the guy said. "But no cigar. Dylan."

He held out his hand to Cooper, who shook it. "And you must be Cooper."

"Guilty," Cooper said.

Dylan looked at her in the same way he'd been looking at the Nash. "T.J. was right," he said.

"About what?" Cooper asked, unable to stand not knowing what Dylan meant.

Dylan smiled. "You're an original," he said.

Cooper nodded. "He is right about that," she said. "So what are you doing here? I thought you lived in L.A."

"I do," Dylan replied. "I just came up for a few days. I haven't seen the family in a while. Besides, none of them know how to fix anything. If I heard Dad complain one more time about that lawn mower not working right I was going to buy him a new one."

"Tell me about it," said Cooper, laughing. "I had to show T.J. how to pump gas."

Dylan leaned up against the Nash, running his hand over the paint job. "T.J. talks about you a lot," he said.

"Really?" Cooper asked, intrigued. Like her, T.J. didn't have a lot of close friends, so she'd never really spoken to anyone who knew him well. She'd sometimes wondered what he told people about her. Now that she was talking to Dylan she figured it was her chance to find out.

"Oh, yeah," Dylan said. "I've never heard him talk about anyone the way he talks about you. Or, I should say, about any*thing*. The only thing he ever got excited about was music. Until you."

Cooper looked away from Dylan's gaze. She was surprised at how hearing what he had to say made her feel. T.J. talked to his brother about her? She knew how much he loved Dylan and how much he respected his opinion. For him to talk to his big brother about her meant that he really cared.

"I guess he told you we haven't exactly been talking much lately," she said finally.

Dylan nodded. "He mentioned it," he said guardedly.

Cooper sighed. "Can I ask you something?" she said.

"Shoot," replied Dylan.

"Why is your brother such a pain in the butt?" she said.

Dylan laughed loudly. "I'm afraid all the McAllister men are like that," he said. "My mother has wondered the same thing about my father since the day she met him."

Dylan was quiet for a moment. Then he said,

"T.J. said he told you about what happened to me," he said.

Cooper nodded. "I hope that's okay," she said.

"He wouldn't have told you if it wasn't," Dylan responded. "So you know how upset he was about the whole thing, then?"

Cooper nodded, not sure of what else to say.

"T.J. worries about it more than I do myself," Dylan said. "They all do. Sometimes it drives me nuts."

"Same here," said Cooper. "So how do you get them to calm down?"

"You don't," Dylan said. "That's what people who love you do. They worry."

Cooper sighed. "But he just won't listen," she said.

Dylan smiled again. "I don't know what the two of you are having a difference of opinion about," he said. "T.J. didn't tell me. But whatever it is, it sounds to me like both of you feel strongly about it."

"That's an understatement," said Cooper.

"Which means that either one of you has to budge or you have to come to some kind of compromise," Dylan continued.

"But how can we do that when neither one of us wants to give in?" asked Cooper.

"That's the hard part," Dylan answered. "I've been in a relationship for four years now, and I can tell you that the hardest part is finding that common ground when you both think you're right."

"Well, I feel sorry for anyone who has to find that common ground with a McAllister boy," Cooper said. "Your boyfriend has my sympathies."

"I'd pass that along," Dylan said, "but I don't want to give him any more ammo than he already has. You made the first step, though, and that's usually the hardest."

"What's that?" Cooper asked.

"You came over here," Dylan said.

"Yeah, well, I was planning on yelling at him some more," said Cooper.

"Well, you can decide what to say while you walk to the door," said Dylan, nodding toward the house. "He's inside."

Cooper looked at the door, which suddenly seemed really imposing.

"Go on," said Dylan. "What have you got to lose?"

"Oh, nothing," answered Cooper. "Just my pride."

Dylan snorted. "Trust me," he said. "You can always get that back. But a McAllister boy—now, that's not something you want to let slip through your fingers."

"Give me a break," Cooper said, laughing, as she walked away.

"Can I sit in your car?" Dylan called after her.

"Sure," Cooper called back. "Just don't get grease on the seats. I'd have to kill you."

She walked up to the door and rang the bell. She didn't even have time to take a deep breath before the door opened and T.J. was standing in front of her.

"You didn't give him the keys, did you?" he asked.

"Excuse me?" said Cooper.

"Dylan," T.J. said. "You didn't give him the keys, did you? We won't see him all day if you did."

"No," Cooper said, holding up the keys. "They're safe and sound."

"Good," said T.J.

"Um, can I come in?" asked Cooper.

T.J. stepped aside, and Cooper walked into the house. Unlike her house, which resembled a museum because it had to be kept clean for the tourists who came to see it for its place in Beecher Falls town history, the McAllisters' home was much more casual. There were magazines on the coffee table, and their dog, a big old Irish setter named Mac, was allowed to sleep on the couch. Cooper liked going there because it always felt like people really lived there.

"Hey, Mac," she said, patting the dog on the head as he ran up to say hello, his tail wagging and his nose sniffing around her feet.

"So what's up?" T.J. asked her.

Cooper sat on the edge of the couch while Mac jumped up and sat next to her, putting his big head in her lap. She stroked his ears, relieved to have something to do with her hands.

"I thought maybe we should talk in person," she said. "It's a little too easy to hang up the phone, if you know what I mean."

T.J. gave her a half smile. "I think I do," he said.

"Anyway," said Cooper, "I've been thinking about this."

"And?" asked T.J. when she didn't say anything.

Cooper sighed. "I can't hide who I am, T.J.," she said. "Not for you, not for anybody. I did that and it made me miserable. My mother didn't talk to my grandmother for a long time because she wouldn't hide who she was. I swore I wouldn't do that, and I haven't. I can't stop now."

T.J. looked at her. "And I can't not worry about you," he said.

They sat there in silence, just looking at each other for a long time. Cooper's fingers kneaded Mac's head anxiously while she waited for T.J. to say something.

"So where does that leave us?" T.J. said finally.

Cooper thought about her conversation with Dylan. In the past things had always been all or nothing with her. She was right and the other person was wrong. She never gave in. But that was before T.J. She'd never felt about anyone the way she felt about him.

"How about a compromise?" she said nervously.

"A compromise?" T.J. repeated.

Cooper nodded. "I can do my thing and you can worry about me," she said.

"I thought you said a compromise," said T.J. "It sounds to me like we're back where we started."

Cooper swallowed. "Look," she said. "I've never

met anyone as stubborn as I am until you. You're right—neither one of us is likely to budge on this. So the best we can do is agree to disagree. I'll promise not to do anything that might put me in danger, but that's the best I can do. And you can worry all you want to. Just don't walk away from me."

T.J. looked away for a moment. "Man, you're a pain," he said when he looked at her again.

"*That* sounds familiar," Cooper said under her breath.

"Did Dylan put you up to this?" T.J. demanded.

"Not really," answered Cooper. "Well, maybe a little. He's a smart guy, you know."

"Don't tell him that," T.J. replied. "He's bad enough as it is."

"So what do you say?" asked Cooper.

T.J. rubbed his head. "You're the one who hung up on me, you know," he said.

"Yeah," said Cooper. "Because you were being a jerk."

"I wouldn't have been a jerk if you hadn't been so mule-headed," countered T.J.

"And I wouldn't have been so mule-headed if you hadn't been so bossy," Cooper shot back.

T.J. broke into a grin. "I've missed this," he said.

"I take it that's a yes, then," Cooper said, refusing to smile back at him yet.

T.J. nodded. "I'll *try* not to worry so much," he said.

Cooper stood up. "And I'll try not to give you

anything to worry about," she said. "So it looks like we have a deal."

"Let's shake on it, then," said T.J.

Cooper walked over to him. She wrapped her arms around him and pulled him close. "I have a better idea," she said as she kissed him.

"Is this a binding contract?" T.J. asked when they finally parted.

"In any court in the land," Cooper answered. "And I should know. My father is a lawyer. Where do you think I got my powers of persuasion?"

They walked to the door and went outside with Mac following them. Dylan was sitting in the front seat of the Nash, looking at the instruments. When he saw them he looked up.

"So how'd it go?" he asked. "Did you do what I suggested?"

"Yes," said Cooper and T.J. simultaneously. Then they looked at one another with expressions of suspicion.

"What did he tell you?" Cooper asked T.J.

"What did he tell *you*?" T.J. replied.

"How about a spin?" Dylan suggested.

Cooper continued to look at T.J. for a moment. Then she turned to Dylan and grinned. "Sure," she said, tossing him the keys. "And you can drive."

CHAPTER 15

"Are those shrimp ready?" Mrs. Morgan was scurrying around the kitchen of the museum, her white apron stained with six different colors and a bowl of peaches in her hand.

"They sure are," Kate said, placing the last of the curled pink shrimp on the bed of ice.

"Good," her mother said, sighing. "Send them out there. These people are hungry."

Kate handed the platter of shrimp to a waiting server, who whisked it out of the kitchen and down the hall toward the museum's garden. The Winter-Pershing wedding was *the* event of the summer, and nearly three hundred members of Beecher Falls society were standing around among the sculpture and the rosebushes, drinking wine and champagne and waiting to be fed.

"Just pray those shrimp are fresh," Kate's mother said as she watched the tray go. "All we need is for one of those people to wind up with food poisoning."

"Relax," Kate told her mother. "It's all going really well."

She was right. Everything *was* going well. The day of the wedding had dawned bright and clear. The florist had arrived right on schedule to set up the table arrangements, and the jazz band hired to play was serenading the arriving guests with beautiful music. Kate wished she could have seen the actual ceremony, but she'd been helping her mother put together salads. She knew that Lily Winter—now Mrs. Lily Winter-Pershing—would arrive soon in her wedding gown, though, and she planned on sneaking out as soon as possible to get a glimpse of her.

Best of all, Cooper and Annie had arrived just as they'd said they would. They were both wearing black, and although Annie's dress was slightly more like what the guests were wearing than what the servers were wearing, Mrs. Morgan had been so relieved to see them that she hadn't said a word. Sasha had come, too, and now the three of them were carrying trays of hors d'oeuvres around the garden, offering them to the guests. Everything was going smoothly, and Kate couldn't have been happier.

"Are there any more little meatballs?" Cooper asked, appearing in the doorway. "Some assistant district attorney ate all mine, and everyone wants them."

"Right here," Kate said, opening a container of

the meatballs and spooning some onto Cooper's tray. "Are you having fun out there?"

"Loads," said Cooper. "My *parents* are here."

Kate giggled. "Well, your dad is one of the movers and shakers in town," she said.

Cooper grinned. "I have to admit, it is fun to walk up to him and say 'Cheese ball?'"

"How are Annie and Sasha doing?" asked Kate.

"Fine," Cooper replied. "Sasha is on sparkling water duty and Annie is doing shrimp patrol."

"I really appreciate you guys doing this," Kate told her. "I'm getting *big* points with Mom. So are you guys. I may even tell her about the class if we pull this off."

"Wait until she's had some of the champagne," Cooper suggested. She winked at Kate and left with the tray of meatballs.

Kate looked around to see what needed doing next. Mrs. Morgan and the three cooks she'd hired to help her were checking the ovens to make sure the chicken dinners were all cooking nicely. The strawberries for dessert were all washed and sitting in silver bowls. For the moment, everything seemed to be totally under control, so Kate decided to run out for a quick look around.

She removed her apron, smoothed the wrinkles out of the black dress she was wearing, and slipped down the hallway. Pushing open the doors, she walked into the garden. It had been transformed since she'd last seen it at ten that morning. The little tables were covered in white cloths, and pink and white roses were everywhere. The band was sitting on a raised platform at one end, and the wedding cake was displayed on a table surrounded by more flowers. It was gorgeous, and Kate felt like she'd never been to an event as perfect as the wedding.

The guests all seemed to be enjoying themselves, too, laughing and talking merrily. Best of all, they were eating, and they seemed to love Kate's mother's creations. As she walked around she heard several people comment on how delicious the food was, and two or three mentioned that they wanted to know who had done the catering so they could hire the same cook. Kate beamed as she looked around her. Her mother was going to be thrilled.

"Have you ever seen so many cute guys in one place?" Sasha asked, coming up to Kate with several empty water bottles in her hands. "I think I've died and gone to heaven."

"And they're rich, too," Kate said, raising her eyebrows as Sasha laughed.

There was a commotion behind them, and the girls turned to see Lily and Jack walking into the garden. Everyone applauded, and Kate gasped as she saw Lily. She was stunning. The gown had turned out wonderfully, and Lily looked like something straight out of a fairy tale. Her hair was pinned up on her head with roses tucked into the curls, and she was wearing a string of pearls around her throat. Jack's classic tuxedo was simple and elegant, and as they held hands they looked like the two happiest people in the entire world.

"I want my wedding to be just like this," Sasha said dreamily.

"You never know," Kate said. "Jack does have a younger brother. Ryan. He's around here somewhere."

"Where?" Sasha said, looking around.

Kate scanned the garden, looking for Ryan Pershing. "He's not much older than we are," she said as she looked. "But he goes to boarding school so you've probably never seen him."

"If he's as studly as his brother is I'm all over it," Sasha said.

"Found him," Kate said.

"Where?" Sasha asked.

"He's over by the fountain," Kate said, pointing. "He's taking a shrimp from Annie."

Ryan Pershing was lifting a shrimp off the tray Annie was holding out to him. As he did, Kate saw Annie say something that made Ryan laugh. He put a hand on her arm and she laughed, too.

"What a hunk," Sasha said. "I can't believe Annie is really talking to him."

Annie left Ryan and walked toward Kate and Sasha. When she reached them she put down her tray. "I'm having the best time," she said cheerfully. "Kate, I'm so glad you asked me to do this. I've met some really cool people."

"Just make sure you're not *too* friendly," Kate

said. "Remember, we're the hired help around here."

"Don't worry," Annie said, pushing her hair behind her ears. "I'm just making conversation."

"You seemed to be doing a good job with young Mr. Pershing over there," Sasha said.

"Is that who he is?" Annie said. "Isn't he a cutie? And really nice."

"Kate, I think we could use some more hors d'œuvres out here."

Kate looked up to see Mrs. Winter standing beside them. "And perhaps some more water?" the woman suggested. "I see a lot of empty glasses."

"Sure," Kate said. "We'll be right back."

She walked into the hallway with Annie and Sasha in tow. "That woman has been a royal pain," she told her friends as they walked back to the kitchen. "First she changes her mind once every six seconds and then she watches me like a hawk. She's the one bad thing about this wedding. You should have seen how miserable she was making Lily during the preparations."

"She looks happy now, though," Sasha said. "A real blushing bride."

"She's probably just glad that it's over," Kate mused.

"Maybe someone should teach her mother a lesson," Annie suggested.

Kate snorted. "I'd pay to see that, but I don't think it's going to happen."

In the kitchen, they loaded the trays up again,

and Kate sent Annie and Sasha back out to the party while she helped her mother. It was time for the dinners to start going out, and with almost three hundred plates to take care of, there was a lot to do. Within minutes there were people rushing back and forth with trays of salad, chicken, and vegetables.

"Go! Go! Go!" Mrs. Morgan said, hustling servers and cooks around as if she were conducting military maneuvers. "Watch the dressing! Careful with the orange sauce!"

Kate jumped into the fray, helping spoon sauce over chicken and arranging asparagus on plates. For the next half hour she barely had time to breathe, and when the last plate went out the door she felt like collapsing. But she was also excited, and she turned to her mother with a big smile on her face.

"You did it!" she said. "Two hundred and seventy-whatever dinners, and they all looked great."

"Let's hope they taste as good as they looked," her mother replied. "And we still have dessert to go. Ready to put whipped cream on top of those strawberries?"

"Whenever you are," Kate said, holding up a spoon.

They got to work, spooning freshly whipped cream over the little silver bowls of strawberries, which they loaded onto trays. When they were all done they got several of the helpers and carried the trays out to the garden. People were finishing up their dinners, and Kate and the others were able to put the bowls of berries on the cake table while the servers helped clear away the dishes.

"Can you ask Cooper, Annie, and Sasha to help hand out bowls?" Mrs. Morgan asked Kate. "They're going to cut the cake soon."

"I'll go get them," said Kate, walking off into the crowd to look for her friends.

She found Sasha and Cooper clearing plates. It took longer to find Annie, but finally she did. Annie was talking to Ryan Pershing. They were sitting together at a table, laughing and having a good time.

"Excuse me," Kate said, annoyed. "I don't mean to interrupt, but could I borrow Annie for a minute?"

"As long as you send her back when you're done with her," Ryan said.

Annie laughed as she stood up and followed Kate.

"What are you doing?" Kate asked. "You're supposed to be serving the guests, not flirting with them."

"I wasn't flirting," Annie said. "Relax."

There was no time to argue with her, so Kate ignored the comment. "They're about to cut the cake," she said. "My mother needs us to hand out strawberries."

As they walked back to the cake table, Annie kept talking. "Ryan was telling me all the awful things his mother and Mrs. Winter have been doing to Lily and Jack," she said. "Did you know they didn't even *want* to get married here? They wanted a small ceremony with just their friends. But the mayor and Mrs. Winter wanted to turn this into a political thing."

"There's a shock," Kate said.

"Can you imagine ruining your own children's wedding just because you're selfish?" asked Annie. "Those two have some nerve."

"Lily and Jack seem to be enjoying themselves," said Kate.

Annie sniffed. "That's not the point," she said.

"Maybe not," Kate told her. "But right now all we're worried about is strawberries and cake."

"But—" Annie said.

"Strawberries and *cake*," Kate repeated firmly.

Annie pouted but didn't say anything as they reached the table. Kate's mother gathered them around and explained what she wanted done.

"When people get their cake you hand them a bowl of berries with cream on it," she said. "It's very easy. But we're going to have a lot of people coming up here all at once so it's going to be busy. Got it?"

Everybody nodded. A moment later Mr. Winter approached them. "Ready?" he asked Mrs. Morgan, who nodded.

Mr. Winter turned around. He held up his champagne glass and tapped on it with his fork. "May I have your attention, please," he called out.

All around the garden conversation ceased as

people turned to look at Mr. Winter. He cleared his throat and said, "I'm delighted that you could all come to my museum today for our little party. I can't tell you how delighted Mrs. Winter and I are to have Jack as a son, and I believe the mayor and Mr. Pershing feel the same way. Now, if the bride and groom will come up here, we can make this all official with some wedding cake."

Lily and Jack walked over and stood beside Mr. Winter, who raised his glass to them. "I want to offer a toast," he said. "To the most beautiful bride in the world and her lucky husband."

Everyone laughed at his comment and raised their own glasses to toast the newlyweds. Then Jack and Lily took the knife that was sitting next to the cake and, holding it together, cut out a big piece. The people in the garden applauded, and Lily smiled as Jack picked up a piece of the cake and held it to her mouth. She took a bite and then did the same for him.

"And now that we're sure it isn't poisoned, the rest of you can have some," Jack called out jokingly. "Come and get it."

The table was quickly surrounded by people who wanted cake and strawberries. Kate and the others were busy handing out bowls and spoons, and it wasn't until she looked up twenty minutes later that Kate realized that Annie was nowhere to be seen.

At the same time the band began playing and Jack

and Lily stepped into the cleared area of the garden to have the first dance of the evening. A minute or two later other couples joined them, and soon the garden was filled with people swaying together.

Kate watched the scene, thrilled that it was almost over and everything had gone smoothly. The food had been delicious, everyone was having a great time, and she was sure her mother was going to be thrilled with how she and her friends had behaved.

Suddenly the air was filled with a sharp scream. People stopped dancing and looked around. As Kate looked on, Mrs. Winter emerged from a knot of dancers, holding her hand to her chest. There was a red smear down the front of her dress, and for a brief horrible moment Kate thought that she was bleeding.

"Strawberries!" Mrs. Winter shrieked. "Someone threw strawberries at me!"

"Who did this?" Mayor Pershing said, rushing over to dab at Mrs. Winter's dress.

"I don't know," wailed the distraught woman. "It just came out of nowhere."

The mayor turned around, glaring at the gawking crowd. She opened her mouth to say something, but just as she did a chunk of cake hit her in the side of the face. Frosting smeared across her cheek and stuck in her hair, and the cake dripped onto her dress. She let out a bellow of rage and started shaking her fists.

All around her, people looked on in horror. Then someone laughed, and before long a lot of people were laughing. While the mayor and Mrs. Winter stood next to one another, their faces contorted in anger, their guests couldn't help but laugh at how ridiculous they looked.

"Stop it!" the mayor shouted. "Stop laughing. I want to know who did this. I want to know now."

The laughter stopped, and the mayor stalked away from the group with a still-crying Mrs. Winter behind her. They walked through the doors and headed for the kitchen, with Kate and her mother following them anxiously.

"I'm sure we can wash that right off, Mrs. Mayor," said Mrs. Morgan as they reached the kitchen.

Kate ran a rag under warm water and handed it to her mother, who started to wipe the frosting off the mayor's face and dress. Kate turned to Mrs. Winter and tried to help her.

"Maybe if we blot it with club soda it will come out," she suggested.

"Oh, it doesn't matter," said Mrs. Winter, pushing Kate's hand away. "Everything is ruined."

Lily and Jack came running in a moment later looking very concerned.

"Mother, are you all right?" Lily asked.

Her mother turned to her. "I suppose this is your idea of a joke," she said. "Trying to make me look stupid just because I wouldn't let you have your way."

"Me?" Lily said, shocked. "I had nothing to do with this."

"Then who did?" Mrs. Winter demanded.

"Was this one of your college friends, Jack?" asked the mayor. "I told you I didn't want those overgrown frat boys here."

"Don't look at me," Jack said. "You cut most of my friends off the guest list."

"Well, if it wasn't them then who was it?" his mother said angrily. "I have been made a laughingstock in front of some very important people. I am very disappointed in the two of you. Very disappointed."

"But we—" Jack said.

"Oh, don't bother," the mayor said. "This is just like you, Jack. I suppose you think it's hysterical. Well, have a good laugh."

"Jack would never do something like this, Mom," Lily said to the mayor.

"Don't you start too, Lily," Mrs. Winter said. "We'll all talk about this later. Right now your guests expect to see you dancing. We already look like fools. There's no need for you two to look the same."

The two mothers looked at their children with stern expressions. Lily and Jack turned and walked away, looking like they were being sent to their rooms.

"I don't know what could possibly have gotten into them," Mayor Pershing said when they were gone. "But thanks to them everything has been ruined."

Mrs. Morgan looked at Kate but didn't say anything. Kate knew her mother was worried that the incident was going to make everyone forget all about how good her food had been. And Kate was worried that it would make her mother forget how much Cooper, Sasha, and Annie had helped out.

Annie, she thought suddenly. Where had Annie been during the incident? Kate hadn't seen her anywhere. *No*, she thought as an idea sprang into her head. *She wouldn't. She just wouldn't.*

CHAPTER 16

"Okay," Kate said. "Spill it."

She and Cooper had found Annie. She was carrying dishes in from outside. They cornered her in the hallway and dragged her into the bathroom.

"What do you mean?" Annie asked innocently.

Kate looked at Cooper, then back at Annie. "You disappeared right before that strawberry flew," she said. "Where did you go?"

Annie's eyes went wide. "You don't think *I* did that, do you?" she asked. She sounded sincere, but Kate saw that the corners of her mouth were twisting up into a smile.

"I knew it!" Kate said.

Annie, unable to contain herself another second, let out a laugh. "Come on," she said. "It was funny. And you agreed that somebody should teach those two a lesson for being so pushy."

"I didn't say that *you* should do something," Kate snapped. "You ruined the wedding, Annie."

Annie looked hurt. "It wasn't just me," she said. "Ryan helped."

"Ryan?" Kate said in disbelief.

Annie nodded. "You didn't think I could be in two places at once, did you?" she asked. "Besides, he thought his mother could use a little pie in the face, too. Or should I say cake in the face?"

Kate paced back and forth. "I can't believe this," she said. "Not only did you ruin the wedding of two of the most important families in town but you got one of the family members to help you? What's going to happen when he decides to tell his brother what happened?"

"You worry too much," Annie said, smiling.

"Tell that to my mother," said Kate. "She's in the kitchen right now terrified that she'll never get another job because of this."

"This had nothing to do with her," said Annie. "It was just a little joke."

"Not when people find out that someone she hired to help her was responsible. Don't you get it, Annie? I asked you to come today to make things easier. But now you've just caused trouble and made it all worse."

"And ruined Jake and Lily's wedding," Cooper added.

"This is it, Annie," said Kate. "I know you keep saying that you're not doing anything, but I just don't believe you. You haven't been acting yourself, and frankly, I don't think I like the way you *are* acting. It's like someone else has taken over your body or something. You would *never* have done something like this before."

Annie leaned up against the sink and folded her arms over her chest. "I'm not a little kid," she said. "Stop treating me like one."

"Then stop acting like one!" replied Kate furiously.

"I'm sorry you two feel like I'm having more fun than you are," Annie said, looking from Kate to Cooper. "It's not my fault that I did the ritual and you didn't, so I don't see—"

"Wait a minute," Cooper said. "Back up. What did you say?"

"I said it's not my fault that I did the ritual," said Annie. "I asked you guys to come, but you were too busy doing other things."

"What ritual?" Cooper asked. "You never mentioned a ritual."

Annie looked away. "Oh, didn't I?" she said. "It was no big deal. Anyway, the point is—"

"No," Kate said. "Tell us about this ritual. What was it?"

Annie gave her a petulant look. "It was just the blue moon ritual," she said. "Remember, the one you guys didn't want to do? I just did one myself, that's all."

"And what exactly did you do?" Cooper pressed.

"Nothing!" Annie said. "Just the usual stuff."

"Elaborate," Kate ordered.

Annie sighed as if Kate had just asked her to list

the principal imports and exports of Denmark. "I lit some candles," she said. "I cast a circle. I did a meditation. I invoked Freya. I—"

"Whoa," Kate said. "Go back one."

"I did a meditation?" Annie said.

Kate shook her head. "No," she said. "The part where you invoked Freya. What do you mean exactly?"

Annie shrugged her shoulders. "I just asked her for a little help," she said.

Kate let out a sigh. "If I recall correctly, Freya is a goddess of love and beauty, right?"

"Among other things," Annie replied crossly.

"And you asked her for a little help doing what?" Cooper asked.

Annie looked chagrined. "Being more like her," she said. "But it wasn't a spell or anything. I found it in this book, and it sounded like a great idea. I didn't ask Freya to *do* anything really."

"Maybe not," said Kate. "But I think she did something anyway."

"You guys are trying to ruin this for me," Annie said. "I didn't do anything. I just asked Freya to hang around a little, and now you're acting like I sold my soul or something."

"Did you?" Cooper asked teasingly.

"No!" said Annie. "Don't even joke like that."

"What did you say?" asked Kate. "Do you remember?"

Annie held out her hands in the air. "I don't

know," she said in exasperation. "Oh, Freya, do you want to come and be my friend for a while because my real friends are all too busy with their boyfriends and their lives, I guess. Or something like that."

Kate put her hand to her forehead. "Okay," she said. "Now that we know what you did, we have to figure out what exactly happened."

"No," Cooper said. "We have to figure out what to *do* about it."

"Why do we have to do anything?" asked Annie. "I'm having a great time. You two are the ones who have a problem with it. Why should I have to *do* something about finally enjoying my life?"

"I don't think you get it," Cooper said. "You're out of control. *Way* out of control. You might feel fine, but—trust me—you're not fine."

"What have I done that's out of control?" Annie demanded.

Kate and Cooper exchanged looks. "Number one," Kate said, holding up a finger. "You've become a fashion plate."

"Number two," continued Cooper. "You slapped Sherrie."

"Number three," followed Kate. "You kissed a boy."

"Number four," Cooper said. "You whipped strawberries at the mayor."

"Shall we go on?" asked Kate. "Or is that enough?"

"Ooooh," Annie said. "This isn't fair. I'm just having a little fun. And it was cake, not strawberries.

The strawberries went on Mrs. Winter."

"Well, the fun is over," Kate said. "I believe that you didn't mean to do anything with this ritual, but you did. I don't know what, and I don't know how it's working, but we have to put an end to it."

"How?" Cooper asked while Annie sulked.

"We'll ask Tyler's mom," Kate said. "Sophia won't be back until Tuesday afternoon, but Rowan is back tomorrow. I'm sure she'll be able to think of something." She turned to Annie. "In the meantime, don't do anything else."

"Does that mean I shouldn't call Ryan?" asked Annie. "He gave me his phone number."

"No!" said Cooper and Kate forcefully.

"What about Brian?" added Kate.

Annie frowned. "I didn't think it would hurt to have a backup just in case," she said.

"That's it," Cooper said. "You're grounded until tomorrow. I'm staying at your house tonight just to make sure you don't cause any more trouble."

Kate looked at her watch. "We've been in here for ten minutes," she said. "We'd better get back out there."

She pushed open the door of the rest room and they stepped into the hall.

"There you are," said Sasha, who was walking by with a tray full of plates.

"We had to have a little girl talk," Kate explained.

Sasha looked interested. "Anything I should know?" she asked.

"Later," Kate said. "How's my mom doing?"

"Well, she's stopped talking to herself, so I guess that's a good sign," Sasha replied.

Kate groaned. "Let's go help clean up," she said. "The sooner I get her home the better."

They all went into the kitchen, where Mrs. Morgan was busily ordering the crew around. The girls pitched in, and soon things were tidied up and the leftover food was packed into containers. As Kate's mother washed the last dish and put it away, she sighed.

"Remind me never to do this again, will you?" she said.

"Come on," Kate said. "It wasn't that bad."

Mrs. Morgan sighed. "That poor girl," she said. "Now whenever she thinks back on her wedding day she's going to remember her mother covered in strawberries."

"Do they have any idea who it was?" Kate asked hesitantly.

Mrs. Morgan shook her head. "Nobody saw a thing," she said. "It was like magic or something."

Kate pretended to be engrossed in putting away leftovers, and she hoped her mother hadn't noticed her reaction to the word "magic." *If you only knew*, she thought silently.

When everything was cleaned up and put away, Mrs. Morgan called everybody to gather around the kitchen's central counter. "I want to thank you for helping out today," she said. "I could never have done this without you. While not everything went exactly according to plan, our end of things couldn't have gone more smoothly."

Kate looked across the table at Annie, who was studiously looking at the floor while Cooper stood beside her, keeping an eye on her every move.

"So thanks and good night," Mrs. Morgan finished. "I'll see you all next time."

The crew broke up, and Kate picked up some things to carry out to the car. At the door, she met up with Cooper and Annie again.

"I'll call you guys tomorrow and tell you when and where to meet me," she said. "Don't let her out of your sight," she added to Cooper.

"Don't worry," Cooper replied. "I asked Sasha to come too so we can take shifts watching her and making sure she doesn't try to get out the window using her sheets as a ladder or something."

"Please," Annie said, sounding disgusted. "And ruin perfectly good sheets?"

"I'd laugh if I weren't so annoyed at you," Kate said. "I'll see you tomorrow."

An hour later, Cooper, Annie, and Sasha were sitting in Annie's bedroom. They'd gotten a ride home with Cooper's parents before walking to Annie's, so Cooper had been able to pick up a change of clothes for herself. Sasha was wearing a pair of Annie's shorts and one of her T-shirts, and

Annie was sitting on the bed in some pink silk pajamas she'd recently purchased.

"Okay," Sasha said into the phone. "I'll see you tomorrow."

She hung up and turned to the others. "Thea says hi," she said. "Now, are you going to tell me why we're playing watchdog for Miss Crandall here?"

"Annie's gone and bewitched herself," Cooper said, stretching out on the sleeping bag she'd rolled out on the floor.

"I did not," said Annie moodily. She turned to Sasha and added, "I did a ritual where I asked Freya for a little help, that's all. Cooper and Kate are acting like I summoned up the hounds of hell."

"Don't listen to her," Cooper said. "She's not herself. We're not sure *who* she is, but she's definitely not herself."

"Is this like *The Exorcist*?" asked Sasha with interest. "Are you going to start spitting pea soup and all that?"

"Hardly," Annie said.

"So what are we going to do?" said Cooper. "It's not that late."

"Because if this *was* like *The Exorcist* we could just throw some holy water on you or something," Sasha continued, still on the subject of the famous horror movie.

"Would you stop already?" Annie said.

"I don't know," Cooper said thoughtfully.

"Maybe Sasha is on to something."

"What are you talking about?" Annie asked warily.

"Think about it," Cooper said. "If you were somehow, you know, filled with some kind of force or whatever that has transformed you into a glamour queen, maybe we can sort of take it out of you again."

"What are you thinking?" Sasha asked.

"Well, look at her," said Cooper, gesturing toward Annie, who was busily painting her toenails. "What if we forcibly turned her back into the old Annie?"

Sasha looked thoughtful. "Hmm," she said. "Sort of a reverse Cinderella's fairy godmother sort of thing. I like it."

Annie looked at them, squinting her eyes. "Well, I don't," she said. "So forget it."

Cooper ignored her, speaking to Sasha. "What if we forced her into some sweatpants?" she said.

"Ooh," Sasha replied. "I like that. And you know what would look *really* good?"

Cooper raised one eyebrow questioningly.

"Pigtails," Sasha said, looking meaningfully at Annie's hair.

Annie looked up, the brush for the polish in her hand. "You wouldn't," she said.

"Oh, but we would," replied Cooper. She stood up and advanced toward Annie. "The power of the pigtails compels you!" she said, imitating one of the classic scenes from *The Exorcist* as Annie pushed herself against the wall.

"Don't touch my hair!" Annie wailed as her friends descended upon her.

CHAPTER 17

Rowan was laughing. "I'm sorry," she said, covering her smile with her hand. "I'm not making fun of you or anything."

"Then, what's so funny?" asked Annie.

They were sitting in the living room of the Decklins' house. Rowan was seated in an armchair while Annie, Kate, and Cooper sat on the couch. Tyler was out working with Thatcher, and Kate had asked his mother to not mention anything to him about what they were doing. Sasha, after staying over at Annie's the night before, had gone home after promising to check in later.

Rowan composed herself and took a deep breath. "What you've done is called aspecting," she said. "You've just taken it a little farther than you probably should have."

"Aspecting?" Kate asked.

Rowan nodded. "Aspecting is when someone takes on the characteristics—or aspects—of a particular deity she or he is working with. Usually, it's only done during rituals where we want to honor a certain god or goddess."

"But I wasn't doing that," Annie protested. "I just wanted to work with Freya for a while."

"I understand that," Rowan said kindly. "You did this by accident. By invoking Freya, you unintentionally brought a little part of her into yourself. The exercise you were trying to do is a great one. You just didn't know the potential pitfalls to watch out for. This was a simple accident, really. It's like using too much sugar when you bake, or working out too strenuously. You need to try things a couple of times before you know exactly how far to go."

"You always were an overachiever," Cooper joked.

"Do you mean that Annie is possessed?" asked Kate. "You know, by Freya?"

Rowan chuckled. "No," she said. "Aspecting isn't possession. It's more like you assume some of the traits of the deity involved. In Annie's case, she was working with a goddess known for her beauty, charm, pride, and seductiveness, so those were the traits that manifested themselves most clearly."

Annie turned red as the others looked at her. She was feeling like a gigantic fool. "So this really isn't me?" she asked sadly.

"Of course it's you," Rowan answered. "You've just been goddessed up a bit, so to speak. The parts of your personality that Freya corresponds to have been sent into overdrive, for lack of a better explanation."

Annie was silent. She was thinking, and she didn't like the thoughts that were going through her head. If she was only acting the way she was because she was aspecting Freya, did that mean it was all fake? Did that mean that none of the things she'd done recently counted? While there were a couple of things she'd just as soon forget about, like ruining Cooper's performance and spoiling the wedding, there were others she was really happy about, namely Brian.

"What happens when I go back to normal?" she asked hesitantly.

"That depends," said Rowan. "Some people who have experienced aspecting find that they retain nothing of the deity's personality. Others find that they've kept little bits and pieces of it, perhaps the pieces they were looking for when they decided to undergo aspecting in the first place. I was laughing earlier because I was thinking of a ritual our coven did once where one of the women decided to aspect Isis. For weeks afterward she kept ordering people around as if she really were this great Egyptian goddess. It was funny because normally she was very quiet and shy."

"How did you make her stop?" asked Cooper.

"In her case, she gradually returned to her old self," Rowan explained. "She did keep a tiny bit of that Isis personality, but in a good way. She was more assertive and less hesitant to speak her mind."

"What about Annie?" Kate said. "Is she going to return to normal?"

"And how soon?" asked Cooper as Annie glared at her.

"What if I don't *want* to go back to being the old me?" Annie said.

"That's up to you," Rowan said. "Like I said, most likely this is just a temporary thing that will wear off eventually. But if you want my advice, I think you should do it the right way."

"Which is?" asked Annie.

"Do another ritual," explained Rowan. "Thank Freya for lending you her gifts. Tell her what you've learned from the experience. Then ask her to be on her way."

"What if she takes her gifts with her?" said Annie.

Rowan smiled. "I know how you feel," she said. "Aspecting, even accidentally, can be extremely exciting. You feel a little bit like you *are* that goddess. But think about everything you've learned so far in your studies. Think about how magic works. Then decide what you should do."

"You mean we're not going to do it now?" Kate said.

"No," said Rowan, shaking her head. "This is something Annie has to do on her own. She started it on her own and she has to end it that way. This is her journey, and only she knows when she's ready to proceed."

Cooper and Kate groaned. "You mean we're stuck with the junior goddess for a while longer?"

said Cooper. "I don't know if I can take another day of her."

"Who knows?" Annie said smugly. "Maybe I'll wait a week, or a month, or a year. Maybe I won't do it at all. After all, school starts in three weeks, and I'd *love* to greet Sherrie on the first day with a little dose of goddess energy."

"Help us all," said Kate, slumping into the couch.

After leaving Rowan's, Annie went to Shady Hills. As she rode the bus she thought about everything Rowan had said. If it was true that she was aspecting Freya's personality, what did that mean? Did it mean that she would never have done the things she'd done in the past two weeks otherwise? Would she never have stood up to Sherrie, dared to go onstage in front of a lot of people, or talk to a guy she didn't know? Had she really only done those things because some part of the goddess was working inside her?

She didn't like thinking that that was true. She liked who she was now. She liked being strong and confident. She even liked being a little bit wild. She had become the sort of person she'd always envied, and she liked believing that that person had always been inside her, just waiting to come out. If she asked Freya to stop doing whatever it was she was doing, would that person disappear again, maybe forever?

The bus stopped and she got off, walking up the

path to the nursing home. *You don't have to decide right this minute*, she told herself as she went inside. It wouldn't hurt to let Freya hang around for a while longer. *Just don't start any food fights*, she reminded herself.

After checking in at the nurses' office, Annie began her rounds of the rooms, making the beds and seeing if the residents needed anything. Although she normally enjoyed doing that, she didn't feel particularly cheerful as she took the sheets off the beds and put new ones on. She felt as if she were being forced to make a decision that she didn't want to make. She knew that Kate and Cooper wanted her to let go of Freya. But she really didn't want to. For the first time in her life she felt truly alive. Going back to her old self would feel like dying. There was no way they could understand that. All they saw was the problems Annie had caused. They didn't know how it felt to become the person she'd dreamed of being. They didn't know what it felt like to have that and then have people telling you that you had to give it back.

Rowan said it was my choice, she kept telling herself. *I don't have to do anything if I don't want to. They can't make me.*

She thought back to the night before, when Cooper and Sasha had jokingly held her down and pretended to exorcise her. They had been laughing, but she hadn't thought it was very funny. Part of her had been afraid that the wonderful feeling *would* leave her and she'd be empty again. While she knew that her friends were just teasing her, she'd lain awake most of the night thinking about how lost she would feel without the confidence that Freya had given her.

She pushed the laundry cart through the halls, her mind filled with all kinds of thoughts and feelings. She just didn't know what to do. She was going to have to see Kate, Cooper, and the others at class the next night. Even worse, she was supposed to prepare some kind of presentation about her experiences studying Wicca. She had forgotten all about that in the excitement of the past two weeks. She hadn't given any thought to what she would do.

She rolled the cart to the next room and looked inside. She was surprised to see Eulalie Parsons sitting on the bed of the room's occupant, Mrs. Bellingham. Mrs. Bellingham herself was also seated on the bed, and the two women were looking down at some small things that were scattered across the bedspread. When they heard Annie come in they looked up.

"I hope I'm not interrupting anything," said Annie.

Miss Parsons shook her head. "We're just talking," she said, scooping up whatever was on the bed and putting them into a little cloth bag. She then tucked the bag into the pocket of her dress and turned to Mrs. Bellingham. "You just do what I told you and it will all be fine," she said. "I'll see you later. Right now I need to have a talk with this child."

"Thank you, Eulalie," the other woman said.

"Don't you mention it," Eulalie replied as she stood up.

"Let's you and I take a little stroll," she said to Annie.

"But I need to make the bed," she protested.

"The bed can wait," said the old woman. "It ain't going nowhere in the next couple of minutes."

Annie allowed herself to be led out of Mrs. Bellingham's room and into the hallway.

"What were you doing in there?" she asked.

"That?" Miss Parsons said as if she had already forgotten about it. "Just rolling the bones. Answering some questions for Gloria."

"What kind of questions?" said Annie.

"The kind that ain't about you," Eulalie answered. "Now, let me ask you one—what was you doing outside my door the other afternoon?"

"You knew I was there?" Annie said.

Miss Parsons shook her head. "No, I didn't. But someone else did, and he told me about it."

"You mean Ben," Annie replied quietly.

"That's right," the old woman said. "Your friend Ben. My friend, too, now that we've become acquainted."

"You talk to him?" Annie asked.

"From time to time," answered Eulalie. "I thought, living in his room and all, it would be the right thing to introduce myself and thank him for the accommodations."

"How is he?" said Annie, feeling odd asking such a question.

"He's doing fine," Miss Parsons told her. "Says to tell you he misses you, but I expect you know that."

"I miss him, too," Annie told her. "Not that I'm not glad you're here or anything."

"That's all right, girl," said Eulalie reassuringly. "No harm in missing the dead just because the living are still kicking around. But that's not what I want to talk to you about."

"What is it, then?" Annie asked, almost afraid of hearing the answer.

"You're looking a little cloudy this morning," Miss Eulalie said. "Walking around with a big old storm of unhappiness over your head. What's this all about?"

"Is it that obvious?" Annie asked.

"Saw it the minute you walked in the room," the old woman replied. "That pretty pink and gold color you've been carrying around is all smudged with it."

Annie sighed. "I did something dumb," she said. "I didn't mean to, but I did it. Now the only way to fix it is something I'm afraid will make me really unhappy."

"Let me ask you something," said Eulalie. "Are you happy now? I mean *really* happy?"

"Yes!" Annie said. "I am."

Miss Parsons looked at her, her big dark eyes

searching Annie's as she peered through her glasses. "You sure?" she asked again.

"Yes," Annie said, less forcefully. She wanted to believe what she was saying, but suddenly she knew that she wasn't being entirely truthful, with Eulalie or with herself. Yes, she was happy that she looked great and had a great boyfriend. But she wasn't happy that these things had come to her not because of who she was but because of who she was when Freya was helping her out. She wanted to earn them on her own.

Rowan had told her to think about what she'd learned so far in her magical studies. One of the biggest lessons was that nothing was worth having if it caused other people to be harmed. Wasn't that the Wiccan Rede that they repeated so often: An it harm none, do as you will? While it was true that she hadn't deliberately harmed anyone through her ritual, she *had* done some things that had caused harm to people. And it seemed the longer she let Freya have some say in how she behaved the worse things got. Maybe it was time to end things before they went too far.

"No," she said to Eulalie. "I'm not really all that happy, but I don't know if it's because I'm afraid of letting go of something or because I'm holding on to that something when I shouldn't be."

Eulalie laughed, but not unkindly. "Child, it's like that old saying goes," she said. "If you let something go and it comes back to you, it was yours all along. If it doesn't, it wasn't yours to begin with. Hanging on to something that doesn't really belong to you is just going to make you unhappy."

"I suppose you're right," Annie said. "But that doesn't make letting go of it any easier."

"No one said this was easy," Eulalie answered. "I think you know that."

"Yeah," Annie said. "I guess I just wish I didn't have to keep being reminded of it."

"I've got some things to do now," Miss Parsons said. "I'm going to be on my way. But you think about what we've been talking about. Then you let me know what happens. Oh, and by the way, Ben's mighty glad you've been using his recipes."

"Tell him the peach cobbler is out of this world," Annie replied.

Miss Eulalie smiled. "Why don't you tell him yourself? He'd be glad to hear from you."

That evening Annie sat in her bedroom. Once again she had lit pink and white candles. She had already cast the circle. Now she was just sitting inside it, enjoying the feeling of security being in sacred space always gave her. But still there was a knot of tension in her stomach as she prepared to do what she was going to do. She'd put it off long enough, she realized. Now it was time to begin.

She closed her eyes and took a deep breath. "Freya," she said. "I want to thank you for hearing me when I called to you on the blue moon, and for coming to me and lending me your gifts of beauty, daring, and confidence. I've enjoyed them, and I've enjoyed the experience you've shared with me."

She paused. This was the hard part. "But now it's time for me to go ahead on my own," Annie said slowly. "I've learned a lot from you, and I will try to remember all the things you've taught me. I hope you'll stay by me and come again if I call you. But right now I ask that you go and leave me to my journey."

She opened her eyes. She didn't feel any different, but she didn't know what she was supposed to feel. It wasn't like Freya had been living inside her or anything. Yet still she thought she should feel *something*. Had the ritual worked? Was Freya's presence still within her, influencing how she acted?

She sat for a while, being still and silent and trying to decide if she'd accomplished anything. How would she know? Would she suddenly be afraid to talk to people? Would Brian not want to go out with her anymore? Would she just fade into the background and be forgotten by the people who had been paying attention to her?

She was afraid, she realized. She was afraid of losing everything she'd gained by invoking Freya. She'd never felt that way about magic before, and it startled her. Now she understood a little bit how Kate must have felt that first time, when she didn't know if neutralizing her misguided love spell would mean losing Scott. And she understood how Cooper might have felt when the Midsummer Eve magic had gone out of control and she'd been afraid of what it meant.

But they both came out fine, she reminded herself. *They both risked losing everything and they came out stronger because of it.*

Miss Eulalie was right. If she was meant to keep any of the gifts that Freya had given her, she would. If not, she would have to find a way to go it alone, and she could do that. She wasn't positive of that, but she was pretty sure. And the more she thought about it, the more sure she became. Maybe those things she'd wanted had been inside of her all along. Maybe she'd just needed help reaching them. Freya had helped her do that.

"But now it's up to me," she said confidently.

She stood up and walked to her mirror. Looking at her reflection, she smiled. "Hello, gorgeous," she said. "Welcome back."

CHAPTER 18

"Are you really you?" Kate asked Annie when she walked in the door of Crones' Circle the next night. She and Cooper eyed Annie nervously.

"I don't know," Annie said. "Let me check." She ran her hands all over her body as if searching herself for clues. Then she held up her hands. "All me," she said lightly.

Kate sighed. "So you did the ritual? Glad to see you're yourself again. Back to normal. The way I wish Tyler and I were." She sighed again, and her attention turned back to Annie.

"But you still look the same," Cooper said suspiciously.

"Not *everything* was Freya's doing," Annie replied. "Some things are staying, like them or not."

"No, we like them," Kate said. "I think."

"What's that?" Cooper asked, indicating a package that Annie was carrying.

"Oh, just my project for tonight," Annie answered. "I didn't know what I was going to do but then I got inspired."

Sophia came up to the three of them, and Annie greeted her warmly. "Welcome back," she said.

"It's good to be here," replied Sophia. "How was everything while we were away?"

"Oh, you know," Annie said. "The same old, same old."

Kate and Cooper suppressed laughter. Sophia, noticing, looked at Annie and said, "Somehow I think things were a little more exciting than that. But I'm not going to ask any questions. Why don't you three come on into the back? We're about ready to start."

The girls followed Sophia into the rear of the store, where the other members of their weekly study class had already gathered. They took their seats and waited to see what was going to happen.

"How are things with Tyler?" Annie asked Kate as they waited. She knew that he was with his own coven, having their Lammas ritual now that all the members had returned.

Kate sighed. "Still up in the air," she said. "We're sort of at a standstill right now. You know, over my not being out to my parents about all of this. I know I promised you guys I would start dealing with that—and I will."

"And T.J.?" Annie asked Cooper.

Cooper smiled. "He's good," she said simply. "But the big question is, what about *your* man?"

"I don't know yet," Annie said, "I haven't talked to him since I did the ritual last night. Who knows if he'll still think I'm all that now that I'm on my own."

"You don't sound too worried about it," commented Kate.

"You know," Annie said, "I'm really not. I learned a few things from all of this, one of which is that I am a *very* cool chick. If Brian doesn't see that, that's *his* problem."

"Are you sure Freya isn't still in there somewhere?" Cooper asked, giving her friend a nudge with her elbow.

Sophia walked to the front of the room and stood there with Archer. "Okay, everyone," she said. "We're going to start. As you all know, we missed Lammas because we were away at witch camp."

There was a chorus of moans from the assembled group as people pretended to be upset about missing the sabbat. Sophia played along by making a hangdog face. Then she held up her hands.

"But fear not. We're going to make up for that right now. As some of you surely know, Lammas is a harvest festival. It's the time of year when farmers celebrated the bringing in of the first of the summer crops. Since there are no cornfields nearby, we thought we'd do something a little different and use tonight to celebrate a different kind of harvest."

"That's right," Archer said, taking over. "Tonight we're going to celebrate the gifts of our magical work. For four months now you all have been studying Wicca. I know all of you have had interesting experiences. That's why we asked you to come up with some kind of creative way to express what you've been doing. Not only are you celebrating the gifts of the Goddess but you're celebrating your own creative gifts. So tonight is a talent show of sorts. You're going to find out a little bit about what your fellow students have been up to and you're going to get a chance to share what you yourself have been doing. Who wants to go first?"

"I will," said Cooper when nobody else raised their hands.

She got up and went to the front of the room. "I've been doing a lot of writing about my experiences," she said. "Mostly spoken word stuff. But as some of you know, my first love is music."

She walked over and picked up a guitar case that had been hidden behind a desk. Opening it, she slung an acoustic guitar around her neck.

"Usually I do the electric thing," she said as she played a few notes and tuned the guitar. "But I've been feeling very unplugged lately, so I thought I'd give this a try. I've learned a lot of things since we started, and there's a lot I could have written about. But the most important thing I've learned is that you're really lucky when you have people you can trust, people who like you even when you're kind of a pain."

The class laughed as Cooper continued. "I have two really great friends," she said. "This is for them."

She began playing, closing her eyes as she plucked out the notes. Then she opened her mouth and sang. "Standing in the circle, hand in hand in hand. Our friendship binds us, makes us strong, and helps us understand."

Annie watched Cooper sing. No one had ever written a song about her, and it was nice to hear someone talk about their friendship that way. As Cooper continued Annie shut her eyes and listened to the chorus.

"As the Goddess turns the wheel and we travel on the path, you walk beside me as my sisters, day by day as seasons pass."

Cooper sang two more verses of her song and then ended, the last note dying away before everyone applauded, Kate and Annie the loudest among them. When Cooper came back to sit by them Annie gave her a big hug.

"Now, don't get all touchy-feely on me," Cooper said, hugging her back. "It's just a song."

"It was beautiful," said Annie.

The three of them sat together, watching as each of their classmates went up and presented their work. Some, like Cooper, sang songs. Others read poems. One woman had created puppets that looked like Sophia and Archer, with which she did a performance that had them all laughing and rolling on the floor. Finally, only Annie and Kate were left.

"I have to go last," Kate said mysteriously. "So, you're on."

Annie stood up and walked to the front of the room, holding the wrapped package in her hands.

She was nervous standing in front of everyone while they looked at her expectantly. *I guess now I know one of the gifts Freya took with her,* Annie thought as she fought her stage fright and tried to remember how she had ever done the performance at Big Mouth.

"I've never really felt very creative," she said. "I've always admired people who could sing or dance or play the piano, but I've never thought of myself as being an artistic type. I'm better at math and science."

She took a deep breath, trying to steady her nerves. "But one of the things that being involved in Wicca has taught me is that sometimes you just have to dive in and try new things."

She pulled at the corner of the paper covering her package. "My mother was a painter," she said. "Some of you have seen her work. Sophia has one of her paintings hanging behind the desk out in the store. Well, my mother meant a lot to me, and so did her painting. It's one of the things I remember most clearly about her."

The paper came off the package, and Annie held her project in her hands. "For the first time in my life I left an assignment until the night before it was due," she joked. "I stayed up late last night finishing this. Well, *starting* and finishing this. I guess I just needed a little inspiration."

She turned her project around and showed it to the group. It was a small painting. It depicted three figures standing in a circle, holding up cups in a toast to one another. The figures were done in quick, bold strokes, one in green, one in pink, and one in blue. The cups, done in thick lines of yellow, stuck out in sharp contrast to the other colors, as if sunlight were gleaming off them.

"I know it's not great," Annie said. "It's my first try at this. I used my mother's brushes, and I think maybe I got the paint on too thick. But it's the thought that counts, right?"

"Why don't you tell everyone what it represents," Archer suggested.

"Oh, right," Annie said. "Well, the three figures are me and my friends, Cooper and Kate. I made us these colors because they're the colors of the costumes Kate made us to wear to this masquerade dance we all went to together right after we met. It was kind of the first thing we ever did together. And the cups are from the Three of Cups in the Tarot. That card had a lot to do with the three of us coming here together. So it's kind of a mix of things."

Now that she was showing the painting to everyone, Annie felt a little embarrassed. She saw everything about it that she didn't like, and she was convinced that they were seeing those things, too. She wanted to take the picture and hide it away so that no one would comment on it and say anything that might make her feel bad.

I knew I should have written a poem, she thought.

Then she looked out and saw Kate and Cooper looking at her. Kate's eyes were damp and Cooper was beaming. They kept looking from the painting to her and back again. Then they started clapping. Everybody turned and looked at them while they applauded.

"Way to go!" Cooper said.

"Woo-hoo," said Kate, wiping her eyes.

Annie looked at her friends. Suddenly a warm glow came over her. It was the same feeling she'd had when she'd done the ritual invoking Freya. *Oh, no,* she thought. *She's still here.*

But something about the feeling was different. At first she couldn't figure out what it was. Then it hit her—it was coming from inside her. It wasn't coming from the outside, like it had during the ritual. It started deep inside her and spread throughout her body.

It's me! she told herself. *It's coming from me!*

It was like a little piece of the magic Freya had loaned to her had remained behind, and now it was growing. Annie looked at the painting and she smiled. She had made it. She had done it on her own, and she could definitely do it again. She didn't need magic to create something beautiful. She didn't need magic to *be* beautiful. She already was.

She leaned the painting against the wall and returned to her friends as Sophia stood up again.

"That brings our talent show to an end," she said.

"What about Kate?" Cooper asked. "She hasn't gone yet."

"My contribution isn't something you need to see," Kate said, getting up and walking over to the desk. She picked up a large box and showed it to them. "It's something you need to eat."

Kate opened the box and picked out what looked like a pale yellow brownie. "I made lots of these," she said. "The past few weeks have been all about cooking, and I realized that magic feeds me the same way my mother's cooking does. So I thought I would make something for all of you. Those of you who have tried my cooking in the past are probably *very* worried right now. But give these a try. I've come a long way."

She held out the brownie thing to the nearest person, then began walking around handing out more of them. "I call these my Lammas lemon squares," she said. "Since this sabbat is about the harvest and eating, I thought it would be fun to make something we could all enjoy. Because the thing I've learned about Wicca is that it's a lot more fun when you have people to share it with."

She handed Annie and Cooper lemon squares.

"Are you sure they're safe?" Cooper asked, looking at hers doubtfully.

"Eat," Kate ordered.

Cooper took a bite as Annie watched. She chewed for a moment and then nodded. Encouraged, Annie tried hers. She took a big bite. The tart taste of lemon filled her mouth. It was quickly followed by a buttery sweetness as she crunched into the shortbread crust, and all of it was wrapped in a sugary taste of powdered sugar.

"Perfect," she said as soon as she could speak.

"They should be," Kate said. "I had to make five pans of them before they came out right."

"She really does cook the way she does spells," Cooper joked.

As they were eating their second lemon squares Sophia came over to them. "Annie, that picture is beautiful," she said. "I know you don't think it's perfect, but artists never do."

"I guess it's not bad for my first one," Annie admitted.

"I hope it's not your last one," said Sophia. "Your mother would be very proud."

"Thank you," said Annie, beaming.

"What are you going to do with it?" Cooper asked when Sophia was gone.

"I hadn't really thought about it," Annie said.

"It should go somewhere special," Kate said. "How about over our altar?"

"That would be great," Cooper said. "That way it would always remind us of each other."

Annie thought for a moment. "If you guys don't mind, I think I'd rather hang it somewhere else," she said.

Cooper looked at Kate. "She thinks Mr. Winter is going to hang it in the museum," she said.

"No," Annie said. "Somewhere even better."

"That is one fine picture," Eulalie said after Annie had hung the painting on the wall of the old woman's bedroom and then stepped back to admire it.

"Thank you," Annie said. "I thought it should hang in here because you are one of the reasons I painted it."

"Me?" Miss Parsons said.

"You know it as well as I do," said Annie. "Don't pretend you don't. That little talk you gave me the other day helped me make up my mind about what to do."

"I just spoke my piece," Eulalie told her. "You're the one who did all the work."

"Well, I appreciate your giving me the push," said Annie.

"And you're sure you don't want to hang this in your house somewhere?" the old woman asked.

Annie nodded. "I'm sure," she said. "It belongs right here. I can see it every day when I visit. And when you look at it you can think of me and our friendship."

"Oh, so we're friends now, are we?" Eulalie said slyly.

"Whether you like it or not," Annie replied. "Don't try to play tough with me. If I could handle Ben Rowe I think I can handle you."

Annie paused as she looked at the picture. "I wonder if Ben would have liked this," she said.

"Yes," Miss Eulalie said.

Annie turned and looked at her. Eulalie's eyes were bright behind her glasses, and she was smiling like a little girl with a secret to share. "Yes," she said again. "He says to tell you he likes it very much."

follow the
circle of three

with book 8:
the five paths

"The entertainment has arrived," Cooper had announced as she walked into Annie's bedroom swinging a bag from the video store. Kate and Sasha were already there, several bags of food sitting on the floor.

Cooper sniffed the air. "I smell lemongrass," she said. "Could we be having Thai this evening?"

"You got it," Kate answered as she opened one of the bags. "Pad thai for everyone."

"Plus some pad prighking, green curry with tofu, and tom yum," continued Sasha. "So what's the movie?"

"Ah," Cooper replied, pulling a tape out of the bag. "I have chosen the perfect film. Creepy yet romantic. No subtitles or Leonardo. Plus, it has some witchy stuff in it. Not to mention Johnny Depp, which elevates it to instant classic."

"*Sleepy Hollow*!" Annie, Kate, and Sasha said in unison.

"None other," Cooper confirmed as she tossed the video onto Annie's bed. "So what's the order for the evening?"

"I think dinner, ritual, and then movie," Annie said. "All in favor?"

The others answered her by sitting down and opening the containers of food. Serving spoons flashed and hands reached across one another, and soon every plate was piled with noodles, rice, and spicy green beans, and the tom yum was splashing in the little bowls Annie had brought up from the kitchen to hold the soup.

"There's nothing like chili paste to wake you up," Cooper said, taking a big bite of the pad prighking with its spicy orange sauce coating the crisp beans.

The others murmured their agreement, their mouths too full to talk. For a while the only sound in the room was that of everyone chewing and making noises of contentment. When the last noodle was slurped up and the last bit of tofu was gone, they all leaned back and sighed happily.

"Ritual time," Annie said. "Can you guys clear this stuff up while I get ready?"

The others nodded and got to work. They carried the empty containers downstairs to the garbage and put the dishes they'd used in the kitchen sink. When they came back they saw that Annie had put the three-legged cauldron in the center of the room and lit a circle of candles around it.

"All set," Annie said. "Let's fire this baby up."

The four of them stood around the cauldron inside the circle of candles. Annie held out one hand to Sasha and one to Kate, who were on either side of her. They in turn took Cooper's hands, so that they were all linked together.

"We're going to cast the circle in a different way tonight," Annie informed them. "I want to try something new. Since there are four of us I want us each to take a different direction. I'll be east, Sasha will be south, Cooper will be west, and Kate will be north. I want us each to think about our direction, the element it represents, and the qualities associated with it. Then we're going to go around the circle, each of us saying a word that comes to mind when we think about our direction. We'll go around a couple of times. Try to imagine a circle of light forming as we do it."

She paused for a moment as they all thought about the elements they were representing. Then she said in a clear voice, "Inspiration."

"Passion," Sasha said, following her.

"Mystery," said Cooper.

"Strength," Kate said, finishing the first round.

They continued, each of them saying a word. As they did the words formed a kind of chant, their voices rising and falling as they thought of different things to say. "Flying, dancing, diving, planting, wind, fire, waves, stone," they said, the words com-

231

bining to create a rhythm. "Bird, dragon, whale, bear, birth, life, sleep, death."

After they'd gone around several times Annie said, "The circle is cast." She let go of Sasha's and Kate's hands and motioned for them all to sit down. Then she took a bottle of clear liquid, opened it, and poured the liquid into the cauldron. Striking a match, she dropped it in as well, and the cauldron sprang to life with bright flames that burned without smoke.

"Rubbing alcohol," she said as the others looked at the fire. "A little trick I picked up in chemistry class."

"Very nice," Cooper said.

"Did you all bring something to bless in the sacred fire?" Annie asked.

The others rummaged around in their pockets and took out the things they'd brought. They held them in their hands as Annie spoke.

"The new moon is a time for new beginnings," she said. "Tomorrow we start a new year at school. We each want to accomplish different things this year. The fire in the cauldron represents the fires of inspiration, courage, and passion. By passing our sacred objects through the fire and stating what we hope they will bring to us as we start this new journey, we're using the magic within ourselves to make what we want to happen come true."

She held up her object. It was a pen, an old-fashioned silver one. "This belonged to my father," she said. "It was one of the few things that survived the fire. He used it to write in his journal. One of the things I want to do this year is write for the school paper. This pen represents that, and I hope that when I write I will write with honesty and that my words will help people see the truth."

She passed the pen slowly through the flames that jumped up from the cauldron. They wrapped around the sides, coating the pen in fire, before she drew it clear of them.

Kate went next, holding up her object for everyone to see. It was a ring. "This is a ring that Tyler gave me about a month after we started dating," she explained. "I haven't really worn it much lately because of what's been going on between him and me. It's a Celtic knot design, and to me it represents how everything is connected. I know that there are a lot of things in my life that need to be connected, and I hope that wearing this ring again will remind me of that."

She passed the ring quickly through the flames, adding, "I hope that the strength of this fire will fill me and help me to do what I need to do."

When Kate was finished, Sasha knelt in front of the fire. "This might be a little weird," she said. She held up a key. "This is the key to the front door of our house. I've never really had a key to my own house before. This is the first time I've ever really felt at home anywhere. So it means a lot to me. I want to bless it because I really want this to work."

She put the end of the key into the flames for a few seconds, looking at the fire with a peaceful expression. When she pulled the key out again, she held it tightly in her hand.

"It's so warm," she said, laughing.

"My turn," Cooper said. She held out her palm. On it lay something small and round and silver; it was attached to a black cord. It was a circle with a five-pointed star inside it. The lines forming the points of the star were connected, and it had one corner pointing up, two corners pointing to the sides, and two corners pointing down.

"This is a pentacle I got at Crones' Circle," Cooper announced. "Actually, I bought it today right before I went to the video store. I've been looking at it for a couple of weeks now, and when Kate said we should each bring a talisman of some kind, I figured the time was right to buy it. As you all know, the pentacle is one of the strongest symbols of the Craft. This one symbolizes my commitment to studying Wicca. And I bought it at the store where we all study, which seemed even more appropriate."

She dangled the pentacle from its cord and held it in the fire. "Blessing this with fire is also symbolic for me," she said. "It feels like I've been jumping into fires a lot since I started all of this, and every time it's made me stronger. I hope this one does the same thing."

She removed the pentacle from the fire and put it around her neck, knotting the cord in the back. It hung just beneath the hollow of her throat, glinting against her pale skin.

"Okay," Cooper said. "Ritual's over. Now let's open this circle and get to Johnny Depp!"